THE PINK ST

The door creaked as she pulled it, and she tensed: she didn't want the men to know she was here. She wanted to make her decision privately. It was stuffy inside, so dark she felt blind, and she could hear a whiffling noise. Something soft and moist touched her forehead and mumbled at it, like the tip of an elephant's trunk. She stood perfectly still and the soft, rubbery thing went higher and sampled her hair with infinite gentleness, separating the strands and tasting them before retreating into the darkness. She put up her hand and touched bony flesh beneath coarse fur. It trembled but didn't withdraw; invisibly alert. She couldn't see the horse, so she couldn't be frightened by him; she could only sense his character, his massive power. Something quite complex was living in that shed, not broken and pitiful as she'd expected, but only saddened by experience. She moved her hand away from the horse's face and he leaned forward to make contact again, brushing his lips delicately against her wrist, as if he knew she was wary and was determined not to alarm her.

"You can have the watch," she whispered. "I couldn't leave you here."

The Pink Stallion

Lucy Pinney

CORONET BOOKS
Hodder and Stoughton

First published in Great Britain
in 1988 by Hodder and
Stoughton Limited

Coronet edition 1989

Printed and bound in Great Britain
for Hodder and Stoughton
Paperbacks, a division of Hodder
and Stoughton Ltd., Mill Road,
Dunton Green, Sevenoaks, Kent
TN13 2YA (Editorial Office: 47
Bedford Square, London WC1B
3DP) by Richard Clay Ltd,
Bungay, Suffolk.

British Library C.I.P.

Pinney, Lucy, *1952–*
    The pink stallion.
    I. Title
823'.914[F]

ISBN 0-340-50240-1

For Charlie

1

Kitty looked up at the house. It was a big, square building, with frilled eaves, like a Swiss cuckoo clock, and the few lights in its windows trembled to the purr of an engine. A board swung from a frame above her head, reading "Balls Farm. Bed and Breakfast. Vacancies", and a small piece of wood with the word "no" painted on it was tucked into a pocket below. As she stood there uncertainly, a gust of wind ruffled the ivy on the house and tilted the board, dribbling water down the front of her coat.

She wondered whether she'd come on the wrong day. It had been a tiring journey from London and no one had met her at the station. She'd been forced to take a slow bus through the lanes, and then hump her suitcase down a steep concrete drive whose surface was as crushed and split as if a dinosaur had rolled down it. She pulled the newspaper cutting out of her pocket. When she'd rung up about the job she'd written the details in the margin – 6th February, 4.30 train – now she read the advertisement again to reassure herself. "Young, fit housekeeper wanted for Devon farm. No experience necessary."

She did actually have some experience: she'd waitressed in pubs, washed up at the back of restaurants, and even worked as a general assistant in Army catering. That had been fun because the kitchen staff had taken malicious pleasure in teasing their customers. "I bet you a quid they won't notice if we leave the fruit out the crumble today," the chef would say, and they wouldn't. Another time he'd made the porridge so stiff you could roll it up into handballs and bounce it on the table. On her last day they'd had to prepare packed lunches for the soldiers and everyone in the kitchen had been particularly inventive. She'd replaced the standard apple issue with raw, earthy potatoes, another assistant had dyed all the sandwich loaves dark green, a third had put cheeky notes in with the chocolate biscuits, and the chef had retired, giggling, to the larder and used sausage meat to make something so rude for the sergeant-major's flask that Kitty wasn't even allowed to see it.

The front door seemed to be swollen shut, and nobody answered when she rang the bell, so Kitty dragged her suitcase round to the back. The ground had a peculiar texture, both sticky and granular, like well-sucked nut toffee, and clung unpleasantly to her boots.

Round the far side she could hear something squealing and the sound of heavy bodies wrestling in straw. She found herself in a wet yard, ringed by square breeze-block sheds, and there beside her was, at last, an open door leading to a dingy room. A pile of ragged coats lay at one end, covered thickly in hairs, a tumbledrier was churning away at another, belching out wafts of sickly perfume, and two pairs of Wellington boots stood tipsily on the step. Apart from that it was empty, roughly plastered, and had cobwebs hanging in strings from the ceiling. The door leading from it was ajar, and she could hear a voice saying sarcastically:

"My heart bleeds for you, Roger, it really do."

She took a deep breath and stepped through.

Two men were sitting at a kitchen table, facing each other, their arms resting on the surface. The one nearest her had the most peculiar face she'd ever seen, glistening skin pulled so tight over fine bones that the lips were permanently bared. The parchment-yellow flesh was tinted like a doll's with brilliant pink cheeks, and the doll effect was added to by the hair, which was unnaturally thick, and fell in greasy black curls over the forehead. The scarlet mouth opened, and the same sarcastic voice said:

"And who's this then? One of your fancy pieces?"

"I dare say it's my new housekeeper," said the other man, getting up from his chair and holding out a very fat red hand, puffed up like a cushion. Kitty shook it and was relieved to find it was pleasant to touch, dry and warm. While a cup of coffee was made for her she covertly observed her new employer, Roger Snell. He was a medium-sized, solid man, with a torso as shapeless and tightly packed as a potato sack. His face was the colour you'd expect of a farmer, a rich reddish brown, each feature in it exaggeratedly prominent, so that he looked like a roughly carved glove puppet beside his doll-like friend. Kitty sat modestly on a chair while the two men examined her and asked random questions about where she came from, and what the journey had been like. When she mentioned, timidly, that she hadn't been met at the station, Roger Snell nodded his head with sympathy, as if it had nothing to do with him at all.

"I'm surprised that bus is still running," ventured the china doll, whose name appeared to be "Pug". "No one uses it."

"Market bus, see," said Roger. "They has to put it on."

There was a longish silence, which Kitty broke by asking:

"Can you give me some idea of the job? I mean, how many people are there to cook for? Is it just you two?"

Pug cackled. "You won't be cooking any dinners for me."

"Pug don't live here. It's just me and Jack and the visitors."

"The visitors?"

"The paying visitors. It's a guesthouse, see, and we has people in for bed and breakfast and a little bite of evening dinner."

"But . . . " began Kitty, too cowardly to bring up the fact that this had not been mentioned when she'd applied for the job. "I thought this was a farm," she finished lamely.

"A farm guesthouse," said Roger, and Pug added:

"A lot of farms is taking the guests now. Farming's hit a bad patch."

"A very bad patch," echoed Roger. "I'll be surprised if we see our way clear to the summer."

"Have you any visitors at the moment?"

"There's two old ladies in. A Mrs Riddler, I rather think her's a bit particular."

"Giving trouble is her?" interrupted Pug.

"Said the bed was too damp. Wanted a hot water bottle if you please. Women." Roger shook his head in disbelief.

"You want to put a stop to that. You'll never hear the end of it else."

"I told her. I said we don't have any such thing, and if you wants it you'd better go to one of they posh hotels up Exeter way. A firm hand, that's all her needed."

"You're right, Roger. That's all they ever needs."

"Delicate, her said her were."

"Big growthy woman like that, you'd never credit it."

Kitty called a halt to this seemingly endless conversation by asking, "And can you tell me what kind of food I'm to do?"

Pug got up abruptly from the table, and clapped a worn-out tweed cap onto his head. "I'll leave you to your woman's talk," he said mockingly, and walked with a delicate, bow-legged gait out into the room where the drier was still roaring and clanking.

"I can't say I'm a man for the housework," said Roger, "but he's an easy house to keep. It's quite a simple little job, for them as can do it. Breakfast and a cooked tea, and a little dab of cleaning. Where's that book of Deb's to?" he asked himself irritably, and got up and began rummaging through drawers and cupboards. Every one seemed to be filled to bursting with old farming magazines, and as he flung them out on the floor he said, "We'll never go short of paper in this house. Why, in Pug's house they has to use the telephone directory to light the fire. I asked to ring the veterinary and I couldn't, he was gone. They'd torn past his letter, see." At last he found a small, hard-backed notebook and placed it reverently on the table. "Everything you wants is in there. That was Deb's and her ran a lovely house, her did. You just do what's written down there and you won't go far wrong. Now, I should make a move, there's work to be done."

He took a stained brown overall from a peg by the door and began easing it over his fat arms, doing a crab-like dance to get the second arm in. Then he struggled with the buttons at the front. Kitty half rose from her chair. "Can I help . . . ?" she began, but he backed nervously away from her towards the door. "They'll come," he said. "I always has trouble with they little devils. Tricky."

When Kitty was alone, she picked up the book and opened it. On the flyleaf were written the words "Deborah May Snell. Balls Farm, Near Wormington, Devon. If this book should dare to roam, Smack it sharp and send it home", the writing rounded and even, each i dotted with a perfect circle. Kitty wondered what had happened to Deborah May; she'd ask, when she got to know Roger better. According to the book the evening meal was served at six o'clock each night and consisted

11

of institution food, the kind usually given to those too young or enfeebled to protest.

Celery Soup (with one Bap Roll and a Pat of Butter on Request)

Steamed Haddock, Boiled Potatoe and Buttered Cabbage

Semolina and Jam.

Kitty read it with growing fascination. Breakfast was a little better. It was to be served at 8.30 sharp and consisted of

Fruit Juice or Cereal

Fried Egg, Two Rashers Bacon, One Sausage, Half Tomatoe, Triangle of Fried Bread

Toast and Marmalade on Request

Pot of Tea.

It was now well past five o'clock, if she wanted to have a meal on the table by six, she'd better get started. She put the book down with reluctance; it had an interesting section further on labelled "Rules of the House" and beginning "No Washing Allowed. No Drying of Clothes. Baths with Supplement Only. Residents will be Out by 9.30 a.m. and not Return before 5.30. No pets . . ."

It wasn't hard to find the larder; there was a plaque on the door with the word "grub" in Disneyesque script and a humorous picture of a monkey eating a banana. Inside, it resembled a kiosk of best-selling paperbacks more than a food store. Every shelf was crammed with brightly coloured packet mixes. There were soup mixes, dumpling mixes, pastry mixes, even a half-opened pack of cream mix hiding shamefacedly behind a drum of custard powder. Freeze-dried fruits and vegetables crackled in their enticing wrappers, and bollards of coffee powder, ketchup and salad cream blocked out the light from the tiny netted window. Kitty decided on Green Pea and Ham Soup, because she was curious to know what it tasted like, tinned steak and kidney pie with packet pastry, and potatoes and swede. There were actually real potatoes and swedes in the larder, huge lumpy sacks of them, still dewy from the rain.

She worked happily at the table in a borrowed apron. The sky had darkened to inky blue, and outside the window was a rectangle of white light through which angular silhouettes of cows, their udders swinging, were stepping and disappearing. She could see her own ghostly reflection in the glass: a small nineteen-year-old, with skin so pale it looked green, and fuzzy hair pulled back by a ribbon. She had a bony, intent face, the eyes speckled hazel, the bridge of the nose slightly crooked, the mouth fine-drawn and tender, with an ironic twist to one corner. If she'd worn spectacles she'd have looked like a humorous schoolteacher – like her father, in fact. On him that face was deceptive. He looked mild and vulnerable, behaved like it nearly all of the time, but he was the sole teacher in his comprehensive who'd never had any discipline problems whatsoever. A rowdy class had only to see his thin, bent shoulders and smooth face to fall uneasily silent.

She was his only child. When they were out together he sometimes played a game that she was his girlfriend, but at home, where her mother was always listening along the corridor, he was just a thoughtful friend. His bedtime stories had never been about people, instead he'd explained how a telephone worked, or described the curious life-cycle of the axolotl. Her mother Kitty loved but discounted, an attitude encouraged by her father in countless small ways. In early childhood she'd rationalised the feeling by thinking – after all, she isn't a real Perret like us, she's only one by marriage – and somehow this foolish logic still had power to convince. Her father was the reason why Kitty was here, on this isolated farm. There was simply no way she could return home and face him after what she'd done.

She remembered the last time she'd seen him. It was

her first day at university; he'd driven her up and helped her settle in, childishly delighted by the little cooker in the passage. They could hear thumping noises in the college rooms on either side of hers, and they'd sat quietly together on the bed, drinking coffee and looking out of the window.

It was a curious view, half of a very old estate adjoining the modern university buildings. Clipped yews fringed a lawn sloping down to a concrete path, and positioned surreally in the centre, beside a spreading oak, were a pair of pillars, the entrance to an old carriage-drive that had melted away hundreds of years ago. It was an Indian summer, the light had that golden clarity that comes only in late afternoon, and excited first-years were streaming along the path, their brilliantly coloured clothes clashing against the orange of the fallen leaves.

Ever since she was a baby she'd been told how wonderful university was, how she must try as hard as she could to get there. It would open a door into another world, one which had remained closed to her father: he'd won a scholarship to Oxford but been unable to take it up because of a family crisis. His regret and disappointment had never faded. They were part of her, too, and those pillars had seemed the entrance to the mysterious new world where she'd be changed beyond recognition. She'd half-risen, excited, and her father had put his fine, bony hand over hers to calm her, saying, "Please don't waste all this, Kitty, promise me that you won't."

It was exactly what she had done. She'd packed a suitcase and left half-way through the Christmas term, hiding herself in the casual world of catering. It was ideal: accommodation was thrown in, there was unlimited work, and employers hardly bothered to ask your name. At the time, running away from an impossible

14

situation had seemed romantic, even courageous. Now, though, she wasn't so sure.

The pastry in her hands was turning out well. It was elastic and creamy-coloured. She lined a dish with it and poured in the two tins of steak and kidney. The contents made her shudder: lumps of pink, fishy-smelling meat in a black gravy starred with fat. When the lid was on she felt oddly light-hearted, and on impulse trimmed it with the words "Hi! I'm Kitty". ("Welcome!" seemed a bit presumptuous – after all, it wasn't her house to welcome people to.) She looked round for a stove to put it in. There were two. A custard-yellow enamel one, which breathed hot oily fumes and rattled to itself occasionally, shaking a length of discoloured copper pipe, and a more familiar electric one, covered in rust. She decided, after some thought, that the electric oven would be a better place for her pie; more reliable. There didn't seem to be any visible way of controlling the temperature of the enamel one.

After popping the pie in and setting the vegetables to boil she looked for the dining room. She opened the first door she could find, and there was a heavy thump, like a bookcase falling over, and a big hairy dog brushed past her legs. It was a burly animal with one ear missing, and it walked with a slow, arrogant swing, its thick hair puffed out round its thighs, so that from behind it looked as if it was wearing a pair of knickerbockers. When she said "Do you want to go out?" it looked at her with an expression full of contempt, and she felt it thinking, as clearly as if it had spoken, "Of course I do, idiot!"

There were clear signs of its occupancy in the dining room: an oval patch of dark hair in the middle of the tablecloth, and a strong smell in the hearth, where a one-bar electric fire sat sadly in front of an arrangement of dried teazles. The room reminded Kitty of a theatre: pompous and red-plush, its velvet curtains trimmed with dressing-gown cord. She sprayed rose freshener into the air. There was a framed sampler above the fireplace, some text in Gothic writing; when she went closer to look she saw it was in fact a laminated board printed with the words: "Will patrons kindly refrain from making toast on the electric fire. Thank you."

Leaning on the mantel, still smiling from reading the text, Kitty sniffed the rose perfume in the air, and the feeling she'd had since coming into the room, that it was familiar, sharpened. Memory slid into focus, and she realised that the dingy grandeur around her was curiously like the room Lance lived in. He had a flat in the university town; two french windows looked out onto a narrow balcony and were, on winter afternoons like this, kept covered by velvet curtains that fell in heavy folds, the edges bald with age and smelling of best quality hashish. The walls were shadowy with antique furniture and the only light came from a low yellow lamp and a coal fire in the grate. And on that lamp, on a circlet of asbestos on the bulb, Lance would sprinkle a few drops of rose essence. That smell, sweet and slightly musty, was to Kitty always associated with sexual excitement so intense she felt her insides coil in a hoop.

The last time she'd seen him she'd gone on impulse after a late lecture. His door was on the latch and he was playing his clavichord. The sleeves of his loose grey jacket were pushed up; the material had a faint stripe, the exact ashy colour of his hair, and he sat stiffly, his bottom pushed out. The absurd pose was part of what she found so exciting about him; a little camp and bizarre. She crept in and knelt down beside the fire. The windows were open, gritty town air pushed at the curtains; the bed, its embroidered cover wrinkled, looked hurriedly made. She knew he was aware she'd come into the room, but he didn't stop playing until

16

he'd reached the end of the piece. Then he paused before turning to look at her.

"I refuse to feel guilty," he said.

"Why should I want to make you feel guilty?" Kitty asked innocently, keeping her face turned away.

"You rang the bell an hour ago, didn't you?"

"Yes."

"So you know someone else has been here?"

She hesitated, decided to be truthful, and nodded.

"It's your own fault, Kitty," he said gently. "You should always ring. I would never dream of coming to see you without warning you first."

"You wouldn't need to warn me," she mumbled, half hoping he wouldn't hear. He spoke very close to her, his breath tickling her ear.

"See? You're doing it again. You're trying to make me feel thoroughly wicked. But I told you, didn't I, at the very beginning, what I had to offer?"

She remembered very clearly what he'd said. At the time she would have agreed to any terms; and besides, couldn't he change his mind? He lifted her hair and kissed the nape of her neck, and she shivered. "Come on, Kitty. Don't be cross. You know I'm very fond of you."

"I've had a horrible hour," she sobbed.

"What happened?" He was undoing her coat now; her skin felt hot, despite the cold draught from the window.

"I waited by the church and saw her leave. She's so beautiful, Lance. So sexy and confident. I wish I was like her. You'd be nicer to me then, wouldn't you?"

He ran a finger down her throat. "I'm going to have to send you away, Kitty," he said. "I've got to work. I'm up to here."

She felt her eyes fill with tears and shook her head to clear them.

"It's no good," he continued. Her eyes were shut, but she heard his knees crack as he sat back on the bed.

"We can't carry on like this. I don't need this kind of relationship. You make me feel so – brutal; and all I want is for us both to be free. Didn't I say that at the beginning?"

"I know what you said," she replied, eyes still shut, voice unexpectedly harsh. "But I can't help feeling that everyone is capable of falling in love with the right person; even you. If you would trust me I could be the right person, I could make it so that you didn't want anybody else, I promise. It's just that," here she couldn't speak for a moment. There seemed to be a storm going on inside her head: migraine crackled and tears choked her voice. Lance waited patiently, she had to give him that. "It's just that I feel men put women into categories. I slept with you too soon, and I told you I loved you, and so you're never going to take me seriously, ever." She covered her face.

He shifted position, sighed, and began to talk soothingly about how they needed a short break from each other, she'd been working too hard and got overwrought. As she listened she became aware of another noise, faint but insistent, echoing his words. It was a little like an alarm clock going off, but with a deeper, throatier quality to it. It wasn't until she was on the bus home, running his words over in her head – "Why don't you take a few weeks off, to think things out? I could even transfer you to another tutor, if that would help. Really, Kitty, you're getting too intense. It's insane" – that she realised what had caused that noise. It could only have been Lance's battery operated vibrator, hidden hurriedly in the bed, and jolted into life by his movements on the edge. Rumbling to itself beneath the duvet, it had given an effortless parody of his steady, reasonable tone. She'd wept with laughter, very close to hysteria. Wasn't it only fair that such an important part of their relationship should have had the chance to speak up and put its own point of view? She had no basis for comparison, but maybe there was something mechanical, even perverse, about the way Lance insisted their relationship should be conducted. For instance, when they were in bed together he often teased her about how prim and buttoned-up she was, yet she felt he did his best to keep her like that: he preferred her shocked and uneasy.

Her gold watch said six o'clock. She quickly turned over the tablecloth and laid it with cutlery and glass from the big carved sideboard. She was only just in time: as she put the cruet on the table she saw the handle turn on the other door into the room, and she skipped back into the kitchen to check on the vegetables. Absolutely nothing had happened to them. Both swedes and potatoes were cold and motionless. Refusing to allow herself to panic, she transferred them to the enamel stove. Then she bent down and opened the electric oven. She could see her pie through the glass inner door, and it didn't look as if it was cooking, either. The glass door was stiff, and when she tugged at the handle, the movement dislodged the rust and smuts inside. A dark blizzard raged within while she struggled with the door, and when it had died away she retrieved her pie, cold and filthy but still announcing with enthusiasm "Hi! I'm Kitty".

It wasn't too bad. The worst of the dirt could be brushed off, and luckily the enamel stove was extremely hot: her vegetables were already bubbling and hissing. She stirred the soup-mix and set it to warm, then crouched by the hinge of the dining room door for a glimpse of the guests before they saw her. She felt it would give her a psychological advantage.

She found herself looking at a woman of perhaps sixty, heavily built and dressed in a lavender jersey and

19

trousers. Her thorax bulged like a giant Easter egg, and there were naked-looking gaps in her appearance: her trousers ended mid-calf, revealing thick tights and brown tweed slippers, and her ginger-grey hair was curled so tight that a cruel expanse of neck was exposed. She turned in her chair and looked straight through the crack in the door, her face a caricature of pursed disapproval.

"You can stop staring at me, girl, and give me my dinner. I've waited long enough," she said with a trace of Scots accent.

Kitty leapt back with surprise and almost knocked over the saucepan of soup. A horrid metamorphosis had taken place since she last looked at it. Then it had been a thin, greenish liquid with a faintly unpleasant smell, like an old gym shoe; now it was a wobbly porridge stiff with lumps. She hastily scooped off the worst of them and thinned the liquid with some potato water. A bell jangled in the dining room; she had to serve the soup whatever it was like. The portions looked meagre when Kitty had finished straining them, but the other old lady in the dining room gave a squeak of pleasure at the sight. She had an endearing little face, snub-nosed like a Persian cat, heavily powdered and scented.

"Soup," she said, in the kind of voice a kitten might have, high-pitched and breathy. She set her paper serviette on the table and looked at Kitty with gooseberry-coloured eyes. "I'm Gillian Biffen, and this is my friend Mayonne Ridley. We go everywhere together, don't we, Mayonne?"

Mrs Ridley's soup trembled as it was placed in front of her, and a few green blobs surfaced, winking, from its depths, like tadpoles nosing for air in a weed-choked pond. She took a miniature sip off the far end of her spoon and instantly coughed.

"I'd like a roll and butter," she said.

"Don't worry if it's too much bother," Miss Biffen called sweetly, as Kitty left for the kitchen.

"It's the girl's job to bother," countered Mrs Ridley. The kitchen only held a choice between sliced bread with a blush of mould or a hard bap that someone had been nibbling. Kitty chose the bap. To revive it, she would put it in the oven. But when she opened the door, she flinched back: a dense cloud of smoke rolled out of the opening, and when it had cleared she saw a ghostly version of her pie, the pastry ash-grey and semi-transparent, tinkling faintly to itself. The effort of ruining her pie seemed to have exhausted the enamel stove. Manic heat was succeeded by a chill depression; the potatoes and swedes had boiled dry without actually cooking, and now even the hobs felt cold.

"How could this have happened?" Kitty almost shouted. "What am I to do?" One of the taps in the sink gave a sudden belch and blew out a gust of steam. She clutched her head until she felt a bit calmer, then went to collect the dirty dishes.

"The soup was dreadful," Mrs Ridley said. "And you forgot the roll and butter. I hope the next course will be better."

"Be fair, Mayonne," Miss Biffen protested. "It wasn't that bad."

"I did not see you enjoying it." Mrs Ridley handed Kitty a bowl with a piece of raw potato displayed on the rim, two green lumps clinging to it like anemones to a rock. "And you've to learn, Gilly, to tell people if the food is not good enough. They will not improve otherwise. You're too soft."

Out in the kitchen, Kitty seriously considered snatching up her case and disappearing into the night, but it was raining and she knew the last train to London had gone. She tried to be positive. There was an electric kettle on the fridge, the kind you fill through the spout. Surely she could use it to cook a meal? She was

21

wondering whether it would be possible to feed meatballs or baked beans into it and hook them out again with a teaspoon when Roger Snell let himself in through the back door.

"Oh Mr Snell!" she wailed. "I can't get any of the stoves to work! This one keeps going hot and cold."'

He crouched down and opened a low enamel door at the front. "He's a woodstove, see," he said quite kindly, his words slow and distinct, like a nurse admonishing a moron. "He *can't* work without wood. You has to keep him topped up regular. If you want him low, like for a stew or a fruit-cake, shut this damper, and if you want him hot, open him up. Simple, it is." He got kindling and logs from a paper sack in the bottom of a cupboard and relaid the fire, his fat fingers endearingly deft, while Kitty, wincing at the very thought of serving such a terrible meal, arranged tinned coleslaw and luncheon meat on four plates. To her surprise it was a success.

"Excuse me," she interrupted Roger Snell as he was easing the pink meat onto his fork with his thumb. "But why doesn't the electric stove work?"

"There were a rat in there, back along," he explained. "Couldn't work out where the cunning little devil were hiding his self – he'd be out nights foraging – robbing bits of this and that. And I come down to check on a cow calving one night and saw him. Didn't he scream when he saw me! Like a human scream it were – knew he was done for. Ran all ways. Up the walls? You never saw anything like it. But I didn't give up. I tracked him down – and he went in behind that there electric stove. He had a nest up between the oven and the grill. Surprising how much wadding and silver paper there is in there. Makes a good nest for a rat, it do. After that the housekeeper – Wendy, her were called – didn't have the heart to use the stove for cooking. But I didn't know he didn't work no more. I'll have a look at him by and by, after tea."

"Don't bother," Kitty said hastily. "I'll manage with

the other one." She poured him out a bowl of tinned rice
and blobbed jam in the middle. (It came in a metal tub labelled 'Red Jam'.) "Do you get a lot of rats on this farm?" she added casually.

"Not now. We did! Last winter was a hard one; we was right out of hay and straw, cleared the barn, we did, before the spring grass come. And do you know what we found?"

"Rats?"

"Hundreds of them. Thousands. Dead, they was. Must have died nigh on ten year ago, when the rat man come and put his poison down. Gone all flat they had, all flat and crispy, like Pompadoms."

It was still early. At ten o'clock the continuous engine noise that rocked the farm abruptly stopped and the lights flickered out, forcing Kitty into bed. It was a hard, damp bed, decorated with flounces of soiled pink nylon. She opened the window and leaned out on the sill, breathing in the damp air and staring at the stars freckled across the sky. It was wonderful to be in the country; nothing could spoil that. As she turned back to her pillow she thought she heard a horse whinny, far off across the fields.

2

"Boy! Here, boy! I know you're there, it's no good hiding." Kitty could hear Roger bellowing as she put his breakfast to keep warm. She'd been at the farm a week and still hadn't met its other occupant, Jack. Every so often Roger would take a page of *Farmers Weekly* out of a drawer, fill it with odd scraps "for Jack" – a cold boiled potato, a slice of jam tart and a couple of pickled onions – and disappear outside. Kitty had decided that Jack was another dog, or a pet pig, or maybe even a slobbering cretin, kept locked up in one of the farm's Nissen huts.

She was too tired to think properly nowadays. At seven o'clock her travelling alarm would start bleeping, but she was always awake hours before that, roused from sleep by Roger Snell. First there'd be a clump clump clump as he stumbled downstairs, making no attempt whatever to be quiet, then a roar as the generator came to life. Next, pop music would infiltrate her dreams, as the milking parlour began to operate, and beams of light hit the ceiling, as if a small discothèque had opened for the morning. Finally, just before seven, a methodical sweeping would begin, mixed with bouts of coughing. As she dressed she'd look out and see Roger's stocky figure slowly working across the yard, scraping cow-dung off its surface.

Kitty needed to be alert in the mornings, because Mrs

24

Ridley held strong opinions on what was acceptable in a breakfast. Sausages, for instance, had to be cooked right through, so there wasn't the faintest suspicion of pink, without being burnt or split. This modest ideal was almost impossible to achieve because the Snell fridge was filled with a fiendish variety of chipolata which suddenly turned itself inside out with a bang, like popcorn. The bacon, too, was odd: thick and red, with veins of gristle wandering across its surface. At least she had the eggs under control. She now knew how to make the kind of fried egg no one could possibly object to: you simply broke it into a dish of tepid fat and left it for twenty minutes. At the end of that time it looked and felt exactly like a plastic fried egg from a joke shop, but it was acceptable to Mayonne Ridley.

This morning there was a stain on the tablecloth, a tiny brown stain, like a black beetle's nosebleed, right in the centre. Kitty couldn't summon the energy to change it, so she hid it under the cruet: two smiling china dwarfs, arm in arm. As she was arranging the breakfast still life – sausage posed beside a soft half-tomato, two crispy waves of bacon, and an egg lounging on a slab of fried bread – she heard the ladies bustle into the dining room. They'd taken to carrying the lounge cushions in there, and all the fan heaters and electric stoves from all over the house, and between meals they'd sit in a fug of scented face powder, playing pontoon and ringing the bell for digestive biscuits and cups of tea. Kitty's life would have been endurable if the ladies had confined themselves to the dining room, but Mrs Ridley derived secret pleasure from watching her at work. Once, while Kitty was brushing digestive crumbs off the stair-carpet, she'd heard a soft intake of breath above her and looked up to see Mayonne Ridley's buff-coloured legs through the banisters. Another time she'd been caught wiping down the toilet; a blameless, public-spirited action, but one she'd been made to feel was as shameful and furtive as masturbation. Mrs Ridley was also fond of occupying the bathroom for vast tracts of time. No water ran while she was in there; no toilet flushed. There was just silence, broken only by the rare crackle of a petticoat as she shifted position from whatever position she'd been in before. Kitty felt ashamed of herself for listening at the door, but she couldn't help it, it was all part of being a servant, this gradual compulsion to become a voyeur.

Mayonne Ridley had another, more puzzling habit. Despite being provided with a large wardrobe and an empty chest of drawers for storing her clothes in, she laid them out in heaps on her bedroom floor. No doubt it was purely to annoy. At first Kitty had patiently lifted these heaps out of the way before hoovering, but as the days went by, and she became more lazy and slapdash – and anyway the carpet wasn't really dirty at all, she was only going through the motions of cleaning – she began to hoover round them, giving the chore a thrill of danger. She knew there was a chance that something might get sucked in, and yesterday it had. One leg of a pair of strap-heeled elasticated trousers had snarled into the Hoover and when she pulled it out it was savaged beyond repair. Every half-hour she thought about that trouser leg with increasing anxiety. Should she confess? Should she hide it? Was she capable of lying if challenged? Sometimes it seemed to her that she just hadn't got the necessary strength of character for this job, or even for life itself.

"Kathleen," Mrs Ridley called from the dining room. (She refused, on principle, to use a diminutive.) "Could you come in and change the cloth? There's a dreadful stain under the cruet. I'm surprised you did not see it when you laid up this morning."

Later, as she rinsed dishes in the sink, Kitty saw that the clouds were blowing away in threads and the sun was out. She felt profound irritation and weariness at the thought of working. So the whole stupid day would continue: laying tables, fetching teas, and hoovering the carpets, which smelt stale and feral, like the armpit of a stuffed bear.

"That Jack!" said Roger, pouring himself a second cup of tea and adding five sugars to it. "You wouldn't think he was a farmer's son at all. Never up in the mornings, never does any work, you can't find him when you wants him. Useless, that's what he is." He licked fried egg off his knife. Kitty had been standing, numb with fatigue, staring out of the window, but even so the drift of his words broke into her fuddled thoughts.

"You mean he's your son?" she asked.

"Who is?"

"Jack. He's your son?"

"Of course he's my son. He's not much blooming good, I can tell you. Might as well not have a son as have him. Dog's more use than he is."

"Do you think he'd like to come in for some breakfast?"

Roger twisted his face up into an unfathomable composite expression, a mixture of annoyance, puzzlement and simply having his eyes shut. Kitty, roused from apathy by the thought that there might be someone else on this farm more miserably ill-treated than she was, took it for assent.

It was odd to see the sun. The last few days had been so dark with rain that she'd begun to feel the whole world had shrunk to the musty interior of Balls farmhouse. Light glinted off the washed concrete, and a small bird dipped down and flashed its wings in a puddle by the wall.

Kitty realised there was no point in calling Jack's name, so she began opening shed doors at random. Behind the first was a stink of hot urine and four calves complaining from a stall whose floor steamed with moisture. Another opened on a space as big as a

27

church, with columns of dusty sunlight falling from a corrugated roof. Machines lay beached here, painted yellow, red and blue, and studded with spikes and claws.

There was an inner courtyard beyond the first, where the buildings seemed older: they were made of faded pink brick, and had elegantly shaped lintels. A flight of stone steps led up the side of one to a wooden door silver with age. Water dripped from the wooden banister when Kitty pressed it, and it shifted uneasily in its sockets. She sat down on the lowest riser, and tipped her face up to the sun. She was tasting the fresh air, eyes half-shut, when she heard a slapping sound. Two big white birds, most probably geese, swayed through an opening in the buildings ahead of her. They had brilliant orangey-pink feet, set so wide apart that their feathered bodies rocked from side to side with each step. An aeroplane passed overhead, and the largest goose paused and observed it attentively with one eye, head tilted.

The other gave a mournful cry and began nibbling at a weed growing up through a crack in the concrete. It looked female to Kitty: there was a submissive air about the way it kept a few steps behind the bigger one, and the lower part of its body had partially collapsed, no doubt from the stress of continual egg-birth, so that it brushed the ground, collecting a crust of dirt. The gander surveyed the yard with satisfaction, and deciding it was empty – Kitty was astonished he hadn't seen her – seized the battered female with his beak and climbed clumsily on her back. Kitty looked politely away, but not before she'd seen the inflamed bald patch at the back of the female's neck, where she'd been grabbed countless times before. The scene depressed her. The goose's position seemed so hopeless: just one of going on and on being stamped on and jabbed at by the gander, and then of laying more and more eggs until her prolapse became insupportable. She was a wreck of a bird, doomed to drag herself round the farmyard until she collapsed from exhaustion. Although she was trying not to watch the two birds, Kitty could tell the female wasn't enjoying herself much. Fancy going on with all that procreation if you didn't like sex!

There was a chocolate biscuit in Kitty's pocket. She unwrapped it and spun it across the yard towards the coupling birds. The gander gave a honk of bewilderment and fell off his mate, who shook herself, releasing a puff of dandruff which twinkled like confetti in the sun. With extreme caution the gander circled the biscuit, trying to fathom where it had come from; his flat blue eye passing over Kitty and again not seeing her. Then he snipped off a corner with his beak and tasted it. Kitty expected him to wolf it down, maybe biting his wife cruelly if she tried to claim a share, but that didn't happen. Instead he gave a series of doleful cries, lifted the biscuit up and dropped it, and the female came shyly forward and had a nibble, exclaiming at the deliciousness of the treat. When she'd finished she retreated, and the gander felt for the last few crumbs with his beak, in a way that left Kitty in no doubt that he'd been hungry too. Perhaps she had another biscuit in her coat. She stood up to get at the pockets more easily.

It was as if she had suddenly become visible. The geese backed away, spitting at the monster who'd magically appeared in front of them. The gander recovered first, giving a high, whistling shriek and slapping across the yard towards her, head low, neck dipped in a shallow S. The female egged him on from behind, honking with approval. Kitty was easily four times the size of the gander, and his threatening display only made her smile. She was enjoying the drama of the scene when there was a blur of wings and something punched her painfully hard on the knee. Sobbing with

29

shock, she ran up the steps and slammed the door behind her. Outside, the two geese congratulated each other on their courage and quick-wittedness. The female kept recalling yet another high point of the battle and provoking the gander into a fresh bout of modesty. She had a deeper voice than his, which was fluty and effete. He hadn't been effete, though. Kitty touched her knee; her jeans were too tight to roll up and see if the skin was grazed, but she didn't think it was. It just felt bruised and stiff. She sniffed. She wasn't going down those steps again. There must be another way back to the farmhouse. She yearned for the safety of her dingy kitchen.

She was in a loft; old furniture was stored here, wrapped in dusty sheeting. It wasn't like the shiny, sputnik-legged stuff she'd spray-polished at the house: wiping dust off a corner she saw inlaid wood glow beneath her fingers. The floor sagged under her feet. She'd tiptoed past a dark, wet patch and climbed over a mildewed sofa when her toe jarred against something; it was a trapdoor, the edges furred with dust. She eased it open and gazed into the space below, where she could hear regular breathing and feel warm air on her face. It was black down there, lit only by thin spears of sunlight, and at first she could only make out a series of wooden walls spaced about six feet apart. She gazed into the soft darkness until two figures swam into focus: a huge white horse lying on its side, fast asleep, light glinting off one metal shoe, and beside it, one arm flung across its back, a man. Kitty could only tell that the man was tall, with black hair. The two figures weren't that far below her: if the horse had been standing she thought she might have been able to lean down and brush the tips of its ears with her fingertips. Trying to visualise this, she leaned forward and stretched out her right hand. Her gold watch was on that hand. It was a man's watch, given her by Lance. Too loose for her slender wrist, when she leaned forward it shifted and slid free into the air, spinning away from her like a meteor falling into space. She reached out to grab it, lost her balance and fell.

There was a terrible moment when she clawed at the air, then she hit something solid and muscular with a force that knocked all the breath out of her. She rolled, bruised, into a bed of straw, and felt the watch poking into her ribs. There was a squeal of surprise from the horse and it reared up into the air, smashing at the wooden sides of the stall with its hooves. To Kitty, crouching in a corner, it looked deadly: its metal-trimmed feet, the size of soup plates, struck blue sparks from the stone floor beneath the straw and hammered the wood into jagged holes. She screamed, and immediately a hand clapped across her mouth and she was lifted up and thrown into a hayrack. She lay wedged there, too stunned to speak, while the horse bucked and gave high, terrified whinnies.

"Ho, there," said a soothing voice, and she saw a dark silhouette clinging onto the bridle as the great horse reared. "Easy, Blossom. No need to fret, no need at all." The man's voice fluctuated in tone; every so often, when the white horse took fright again, it would lift a register and become a shade louder, then, as the animal calmed and began huffing loudly through its nose, drop to a hypnotic murmur. When the horse was quiet the man smoothed its mane. "It's all over, Blossom. Gently now. No one means you any harm. You keep quiet, hey? Calm and quiet." Kitty liked the way he was so kind to his horse. His voice was making her feel relaxed, too, when she was suddenly lifted out and dumped beside a door.

"What do you think you're about? Dropping on a horse and screaming at it; I've never seen anything so pissing stupid."

Kitty didn't say anything. When he'd first opened the

31

door and let in the sun she'd seen his clothes were old and muddy and roughly mended here and there with big stitches of thread. He was so tall she had to tip her head right back to see his face. It was unexpectedly beautiful, with wide, dark eyes, an aquiline nose, and an almost feminine sweetness to the mouth and the curve of the jaw.

"I'm sorry, I didn't mean to . . . " she finally said, when he'd stopped talking and seemed to expect a reply.

"Grockles!" He sighed and put a hand up to his forehead. "Just get out, will you? I've to see to the mare, I haven't time to gab to you." He pushed Kitty gently out into the yard and slammed the door behind her. She stayed there until she heard his voice murmur to the horse again. That must have been Jack. It was his eyes that had impressed her most; their tapered black brows gave them an exaggeratedly fierce look, like the eyes of an owl.

She could hardly sleep that night for worrying about her great crime. Roger Snell seemed to be suffering from a guilty conscience too. Every couple of hours he'd give a sudden snort, clearly audible through the thin walls, and clatter downstairs. Doors would bang and the generator come on with a roar, and just as Kitty was drifting into a fitful dream composed of Jack's accusing eyes and the white mare's hooves dancing in the air, the front door would creak and she'd hear Roger sighing and dragging himself up the stairs again. At one point she heard the two ladies muttering, but their voices were drowned out by Roger's snores. He snored in two distant timbres, low and high, like a conversation between a road drill and a whimpering puppy.

When she took the fried breakfasts in she had a surprise. The ladies had lost their usual dapper, powdered look. Miss Biffen appeared to be wearing a shower-cap on her head, and her skin was so thickly covered in grease that she resembled a slug rather than a kitten, while Mayonne Ridley had on a padded housecoat, and her hair was twisted onto soiled puffs of cotton wool. Without makeup her face was curiously featureless, even benevolent.

"Can you give us an explanation of Mr Snell's behaviour last night?" she asked stiffly, but her words didn't have much impact, coming from a face without sharp focus.

Kitty yawned. "I don't understand it myself. Wasn't it awful?" She caught sight of herself in the tiny mirror winking among the scrollwork at the top of the sideboard. Her hair was sticking out on one side; she'd forgotten to brush it. She reached up a hand to pat it flat and the tray almost slid from her grasp.

Miss Biffen steadied it, and said: "Perhaps he's ill. I've heard gentlemen often do have problems in the night . . . "

"I'll have no lewd talk at this table," snapped Mayonne.

Kitty was so tired she sat in one of the chairs and rested her arms on the cloth. She no longer cared what the two ladies thought.

"I don't think he's ill," she said. "He looks terribly healthy to me. It must be something to do with the farm."

"Whatever it is, it is very inconvenient for his guests. When I accepted this accommodation I didn't expect to have my sleep disturbed."

"Why should he walk up and downstairs groaning to himself if it was to do with the farm?" Miss Biffen's bath-cap bobbed with sincere interest.

"Well . . . " began Kitty, "he could have some extra milking to do, or . . . I really haven't the faintest idea," she finished lamely. "I've never been on a farm before." This admission softened the atmosphere, and the three of them had a cosy discussion about the more disagreeable aspects of life at Balls Farm. Mrs Ridley described the smell that oozed in through her window in the mornings, and a monstrous bluebottle she'd found scuttling up the side of her wardrobe, while Miss Biffen complained about the way mud sausaged in through the eyelets of her lace-up shoes.

"And I hate the animals following me when I try to take a walk. There are some little cows out there that keep crowding up behind me all the time and breathing on my hair. I think Mr Snell ought to train them to keep away."

Roger didn't come in for his breakfast so Kitty gave it to his dog instead. The two old ladies went back to bed, and there was so little to do with them out of the way and Roger mysteriously vanished that she retreated upstairs too, and slipped fully dressed between her nylon sheets.

She woke to find the light had drained from the room. Her throat felt dry, but it was so pleasant being warmly in bed in the afternoon that she was reluctant to get up for a drink. Her great crime didn't seem so unforgivable now. Surely people fell accidentally on top of horses all the time on farms? It was stupid to put a trap door above a stable anyway, that sort of thing was bound to happen. She composed a brief but telling speech of apology and justification in her head to deliver when she next saw Jack. Their misunderstanding would then be cleared up, and they could become friends.

There wasn't a sound from below; she got out of bed and walked to the head of the stairs, and just before she reached it saw Roger's door ajar. She hadn't been in there to clean – it had seemed disrespectful to intrude on her employer's privacy – but she saw now that it was a poky room, decorated in heavy embossed gold paper gone green from damp round the window. The bed, its blankets and sheets twisted into a rope and half on the floor, was surrounded by open newspapers, and something red stuck out from underneath them. It was a photograph album; Kitty could hardly make out the contents in the dim light, but she saw old black and white prints of severe-looking people in overcoats beside the sea, and a series of aerial views of Balls Farm with 'sample only' stamped across them, showing a pretty white cottage in a wooded valley gradually becoming hemmed in by concrete and corrugated iron. There was a wedding photograph, too, showing an ill-assorted couple on a church porch. The man was obviously Roger, only with wavy hair growing low down on his forehead. He was in a tight suit, arms hanging like bananas, gazing wistfully at his bride: a big woman, at least a foot taller than him, with a full bosom and dark hair wound round her head in plaits. Her face was a surprise to Kitty, after the primly disapproving book of rules downstairs. It was angular and sensual, the long dark eyes tilting with amusement, the mouth half-open to reveal prominent teeth. Hair was escaping from the plaits and curling round her forehead, and this, together with the strong eyebrows, gave her a tigerish look. Kitty remembered a story she'd once read about a beautiful woman with thick fur beneath her clothes and a tail that thumped under her skirt when she was angry. Deborah May looked exactly as she'd imagined that woman; she was even as carefully dressed: in a high-necked, long-sleeved frock, solid with ruffles and lace.

Further on in the book were random groups of farm animals – a bull looking indignant and a collection of blurred cows squinting into the sun – Roger, photographed on a tractor from every conceivable angle, and a small boy holding a monkey on his lap. He was looking gravely into the camera, hair cut so it stuck up in tufts, a painted backdrop of a circus behind him. It was definitely Jack, a sweeter, more endearing version of him; Kitty recognised his almond eyes and wide mouth with a curl to the edge of the lip. She flipped on through the album and stopped suddenly at a picture of a conifer beside a corner of a house. Jack, only a year or two older than in the last picture, was holding the hand of a man half in shadow. A man with wide shoulders and dark hair. He wasn't Roger, and there was an odd intimacy in their pose. Kitty held the book up to the light, wondering why she found that particular photograph so arresting. There was a fierceness about the way both of them were standing, as if they knew they shouldn't be holding hands but were determined to go ahead with it all the same. There were no more photographs. Disappointed, she tucked the album back under the papers.

When she got downstairs the two ladies were sitting up in the dining room, waiting for her, hair brushed and carefully painted faces pink from exercise. They'd walked up to the village, since the afternoon had turned out so fine, and eaten a cream tea in the pub. They'd been overwhelmed by the publican's wife.

"A delightful creature, so smart and well-groomed," Miss Biffen squeaked, and Mrs Ridley retailed in detail a long conversation she'd had with this paragon about the breeding and showing of Airedale terriers. "And it wasn't just any old jam she gave us," she added menacingly, "but real home-made strawberry jam and proper Devon cream. I'm surprised there isn't any cream on a dairy farm like this." She swivelled her head in silent survey of the dismal, stuffy room. "It was a pleasure to be in that saloon bar," she said. "Which is more than I could say for some places I could mention."

3

A mass of angry animals hooted and wailed, over and over again. Kitty sat up in bed. The cows were mooing outside, and more faintly she could hear a baby crying. It wasn't quite six o'clock. She tiptoed downstairs and opened the kitchen door. Roger Snell was sitting at the table, head back and mouth open, fast asleep, a half-eaten sandwich in his hand. She hadn't seen him to talk to for two days: instead he'd been a ghostly presence half-glimpsed through driving rain on the wrong side of a window. The baby noise was coming from a bundle of sacking next to the stove. Kitty unwrapped it and found a tiny lamb that looked as if it had been dipped in a mixture of snot and blood and baked. Its wool crackled under this disagreeable coating, and it opened its mouth and blared at her. She didn't know anything about animals, but it was clear that this one was hungry, so she improvised with a teaspoon and a saucepan of warm milk, tipping a few drops down its throat while it spluttered and baaed, like a drowning man surfacing to cry for help. The row woke Roger, who turned and gazed blankly at them for a while, his eyes marbled with fatigue.

"Milking," he said, and pulled himself to his feet, moving with infinite slowness. Over by the back door he staggered and slipped down the wall, and fell instantly asleep again. The cows mooed desperately out beyond the yard and the lamb lifted its voice and joined in. There was nothing to be done but find Jack. Kitty quite looked forward to seeing him again, and he was the only person who could milk the cows for Roger and help her feed the lamb. She went to get her coat and the lamb skipped after her, dragging its sacking behind it. On impulse, she picked it up and stuffed it down her front. It struggled there until it found a button it could suck.

It was grey and damp outside, and the stable was deserted. Kitty toured the farm buildings without finding Jack, and wherever she went she seemed to provoke intense annoyance in the animal population. The sound of her step outside the long blockhouse beyond the dairy triggered off mass screaming from within, and in a field further on a gang of sheep galloped up and tried to push her over. She was about to retreat in tears when she saw a thin spiral of smoke floating up from behind a clump of trees. She skirted a filthy, open-sided barn with bellowing cows in it and found herself looking at a small shed, its wood black with algae. The smoke was coming from a tin pipe wedged in the roof. If it hadn't been for the smoke, Kitty would have assumed she was looking at a chicken house, but it didn't seem likely that a chicken would have the wit to light a fire. The lamb wriggled inside her coat and she remembered what she'd come for and banged on the door.

"I'm not in," came Jack's voice. "Piss off."

Kitty knocked again, and when that had no effect, shouted, "It's urgent! Your dad's ill."

The door opened a few inches and Jack appeared in the gap, a lock of black hair falling across his eyes. He was wearing a white T-shirt and jeans so dirty they looked brown.

"Clear off," he said, with great distinctness, baring

38

even, white teeth. "I've nothing to say to you; just leave me be."

"But you've got to come," Kitty cried. "Your dad needs you." The door started to close. "Think of the animals," she shrieked, as it slammed shut. "Nothing's been fed, and the cows are making an awful noise. I don't know what to do; I don't even know what they eat." She heard a bolt slide home and rattled the handle.

"That's terrific!" she bawled hoarsely, her normal timidity forgotten. "Great! Well, it may be pretty bad to fall accidentally on top of someone else's horse, but I don't see it's any better letting a load of helpless animals starve to death just because you happen to be a mean, hard-hearted . . . " She paused to search for a suitable insult, but the lamb beat her to it, and blared a torrent of abuse at the door, venting all its irritation at being left on a cold kitchen floor, force-fed by an idiot, and stuffed down the front of a jumper.

The door opened and Jack said wearily, "Hand it over, then."

Kitty pulled out the indignant lamb and he held it in his hands. He nodded. "So he's changed his tune now lambing's started, and wants me after all. Well, you can tell him I won't do anything unless he ups the ante. No chance. I'm not working all hours for a couple of quid. He can bloody well give me a decent wage." He inclined his head towards the lamb. "Has he had some grub?"

"Not really," she answered. "I tried to feed him with a spoon, but it didn't really work. He kept spitting it out again."

"Yeah, well, he wants colostrum, see, ordinary milk's no good. Where's the ewe?" he asked, pronouncing it so it rhymed with "toe".

"The what?"

"The ewe. The sheep that had him."

"I don't know. I just came downstairs and found your

39

dad asleep on the table and that thing crying by the stove."

"So the old man didn't send you?"

"No. He's asleep. I don't think he's been to bed for three days."

Jack combed his fingers through his hair. "I'm not going to help if he hasn't asked me to."

"Couldn't you just this once? Please?"

"No. He'll have to sort it out on his own. You tell him when he wakes up: he can have me back any time he wants, long as he pays me four pound an hour. And I'm not touching nothing till I has that in writing." He slammed the door, but to Kitty's relief he took the lamb with him.

The dairy was hissing when she got back, and she could see Roger staggering about inside. A little later there was a crash as a bucket went spinning; she kept glancing nervously out of the window, expecting to see him collapsed in the yard, but he kept on his feet. She wasn't looking forward to passing on Jack's message; she had to steel herself to bring the subject up at tea-time.

Roger was deep in thought, scooping up beans in slow motion.

"Mr Snell. You know this morning there was a lamb here?" she began, in a light, gossipy tone.

He frowned. "He's out under the lamp," he said. "Can't remember putting him there for the life of me. I'd have sworn he was in here by the fire." He pushed an eyelid up with one finger, and looked woozily at her. "He was pretty near gone back along, but he's right now. Took it hard, see, being born. Got his head stuck half out of the ewe's backside, and it was all swole up; his tongue was like a black ball in his face. It was my doing: I wasn't there soon enough. Another hour and I'd have lost the both of them." He relapsed back into gloomy silence.

Kitty tried again. "It seems an awful lot of work, running this farm. Couldn't you get Jack to help you?"

"Jack? He's no help."

"Supposing you paid him a bit more money . . ." Kitty was about to suggest the magic figure of four pounds when Roger burst out:

"Money! That's Jack all over, that is. Wages for this and wages for that. A day off here and a weekend off there. He'll be wanting a fancy holiday off abroad next. You can't run a farm with days off and holidays! He's no farmer's son – why, when I was his age I was out there all hours and all weathers. I didn't expect to be paid. It was enough that it was my land and I was to have it after my father was gone. Where do the cash come from, if not from the farm? I'd like to know what would happen if I took four pound for every hour I worked."

The two ladies began hiking round the neighbourhood each morning and finishing with a cream tea in Mrs Pugh's saloon bar. The correct costume was essential. After much anxious discussion they bought two raspberry anoraks from the village shop and zipped each other tightly into them. Mrs Ridley had taken to wearing the elasticated trousers with the snarled leg, and Kitty couldn't decide whether she genuinely hadn't noticed the damage or was hoping the sight of it would jolt the person responsible into breaking down and confessing. (Kitty had a story already prepared, if challenged, about how she'd seen the Snell dog bounding down the stairs with a guilty look on its face.) With the ladies away, Kitty found herself with hours of leisure. She began by being conscientious – changing the nylon bedlinen so everyone had lemon sheets instead of magenta ones, and baking batches of fairy cakes – went through a phase of sleeping as much as possible, and finally became bored and restless. On the second day she gave herself a beauty treatment:

snipped a few chunks of hair off with a pair of pinking shears she found in the lounge, and spent the whole of a radio play plucking her eyebrows until they'd entirely disappeared. Her face looked strangely bland without them, so she powdered and lipsticked it with Miss Biffen's cosmetics, in an attempt to resemble the famously well-groomed Mrs Pugh. She'd quite looked forward to astonishing everyone with her glamour that tea-time, but none of them noticed any difference. Mrs Ridley and Miss Biffen were poring over some book on the history of show dogs, and Roger was numb from lambing. He'd put an old mattress down beside the dog, so he could be up and down in the night without the bother of climbing the stairs, and all the colour had faded from his face. Now he pushed his dish of Angel Delight away untasted and laid his head on the table.

When she was sure he was asleep Kitty went out to see the lambs. They weren't hard to find: all the sheep were in the big barn where she'd first seen machinery stored. It sounded like a dressing station in the aftermath of a great battle in there; the air rang with cries and moans. Some kind of system was operating, but it was hard for her to work out what it was. The space had been divided up with makeshift barriers: wooden pallets, straw bales and gates. Here were ewes so grotesquely distorted by pregnancy that they looked as if they were carrying saddlebags; there a lamb on its own, trembling under a low lamp; in other pens mothers and babies were herded in groups or singled out individually. Kitty noticed at once that none of them had any water to drink, and, glad to find something useful to do at last, began filling buckets at a tap by the door. It reminded her of a fairy tale she'd been obsessed by as a child, where the heroine passed through an enchanted land full of unfinished work – an oven that cried out to be emptied; an apple tree whose fruit wailed to be picked – and only had to complete it in order to be rewarded. In the story the work came to an end, but that didn't seem possible here: when the sheep had enough water they called for hay, and when that was supplied they discovered an urgent need for a gynaecologist.

Kitty was leaning over a pen and trying to comfort a fat ewe baaing with distress when she sensed someone behind her. She turned round and saw Jack hunched into a jacket, a hat pulled low over his eyes.

"I think she's in pain," she said.

He shrugged. "That's Cankerlug," he replied. "She always has big singles and they gets stuck. One leg back and she can't squeeze them out. Right plonker, she is." He tipped his hat lower. "Where's the old man to?"

"He's asleep in the kitchen. I did ask him about the four pounds . . . "

"He's not biting, is he? It don't matter anyway." He sounded disappointed. Cankerlug gave a miserable whimper and strained with internal pain. "Can't you do something for her?" begged Kitty.

"I'm not getting caught like that. It'd be giving in, doing what he wants, wouldn't it? If he catches me lambing I'll be right back where I started. I might as well not have bothered in the first place." He cast a careful look over the rest of the sheep and turned to go.

"But you can't leave her," Kitty pleaded.

"Who says I can't?"

Kitty was almost in tears over the plight of the elderly sheep. She saw now that it did have a peculiar ear: swollen to the size of a new potato and pierced by a row of punctures, as if it had been bitten. "Look," she said, "supposing I did whatever it is you have to do, and you just stood there and gave me instructions?"

"You having me on?" Jack laughed. "You don't just make a few passes over her with your hands. You has to get them in right up to the armpit."

"I don't mind," said Kitty, minding horribly. She

43

swallowed. "I'm not squeamish. I've done plenty of disgusting things in my life."

"You look like it and all."

She turned her back on Jack with dignity and climbed into the pen, aware that her jeans were too tight. It was true she wasn't squeamish. You couldn't be if you wanted to work in kitchens. She'd scrubbed out dustbins grey with maggots, squished three hundred soft-boiled eggs with her fingers, and been the only assistant who could bear to help when the poultry chef brought down his cleaver on his thumb instead of a poussin. She'd always found such horrors were best faced as quickly as possible; and it helped to take a deep breath, so you couldn't smell anything.

"Right," she said nasally, "what do I do?"

Jack leaned over the pen. "Lift up her tail and let me have a look."

Kitty raised the stumpy tail with two fastidious fingers. Below was a swollen pink opening with something hard and black sticking out, like a mouth pursed to spit a prune stone. She shut her eyes and shuddered.

"There you are, it's as I said. She's got a lamb with a leg back. There's the other hoof."

Kitty opened her eyes. It was a hoof; a glossy baby one. As she watched, the flesh round it pulsed and the sheep groaned. "So what do I do?"

"You stick your hand in and feel round for the other one. He'll be cocked back like this." Jack bent his arm at the elbow and twisted it behind him.

"Won't it hurt her?"

"What do you think? If it bothers you, don't do it. I'm not forcing you."

Intensely annoyed by his attitude – if it was her farm she wouldn't let the sheep suffer – Kitty took off her sweater and rolled up her sleeve. Then, very gingerly, she put her fingers round the hoof and pushed. Her hand slid inside. It wasn't nearly as unpleasant as she'd imagined. It was warm and moist, and smelled only a little musky. The ewe struggled and gave a loud baa, and Jack vaulted the pen and held it still.

"I didn't think you was serious!"

"I'm serious," Kitty replied, looking him straight in the eye. She marvelled again at how attractive he was. He wasn't her physical type; her only lover had been a small, fine-featured intellectual, but if Jack hadn't had such a beautiful face she certainly wouldn't have ended up here, with her hand inside a sheep. She wasn't sure whether she liked him – he was too crude, some of the things he said made her flinch with distaste – but there were moments when she almost admired him; like now, when, his voice low and concerned, he said: "You've to feel back for the other leg and pull it forward. Cup your fingers round the hoof first, or you'll tear her. It's bloody sharp."

Kitty screwed up her eyes to concentrate. It was a tight, miserable world in there, full of slithery woolly things packed impossibly close together. Her fingers slipped into a wet crack, where they were mumbled by two bands of gum. She felt a tongue flicker.

"It bit me!"

"They does that." Jack was holding the ewe still, his head on one side and a distant expression in his dark eyes, as if he was listening. She felt deeper, round the other leg, and slowly eased it forward until it was lined up with the first.

"I've got them both."

"Good." Jack's eyes focused again. "Now you've to make sure the head's down, like the lamb was going to dive off a swimming pool."

"Then what?"

"Pull."

"Supposing I've got the wrong leg? There're three to choose from, aren't there?"

"I knew I'd have to do it come the finish," Jack sighed, but he seemed more pleased than annoyed.

Kitty gripped the ewe's wool, her blood-stained arm rapidly cooling, while Jack knelt and eased his hand inside. The sheep gave the closest a baa could come to a scream, there was a wet noise, and a lamb slid out on the straw. Jack gave its nose a wipe with the front of his shirt and pushed it up by the ewe's head.

"She's a good mother, Cankerlug," he said, cleaning off his arm with a handful of hay. "Pigging useless at pushing her lambs out, but we can't all be perfect."

Kitty sat back on her heels and watched the mother and baby together. Cankerlug gave a deep purring rumble and licked delicately at the sticky white head, as if she didn't like the taste much but was determined to do her duty. The lamb lifted its head and shook it, so its ears slapped, then, giving a tiny high-pitched baa, like a wasp buzzing in a bottle, felt for the place where the warm tongue was coming from.

"Isn't it lovely?" exclaimed Kitty. "Would it have died if we hadn't helped it?"

"No." Jack smiled. "He'd have been all right for an hour or two. The ewe was vexed, but she wasn't in any danger; she could have waited." He sprayed the lamb's torn red umbilicus with purple liquid from a can. "I may have had it up to here with the old man, but I wouldn't let his stock come to any harm."

Kitty swallowed. "I'm really sorry about hurting your horse," she said quickly. "I didn't mean to frighten her. It was an accident." She smiled, anxious to please.

Jack didn't smile back. He straightened and put the can back in the wall, where there was a brick missing. "You wouldn't understand what you'd done if I told you," he said.

"I could try." He looked at her.

"See these sheep?" he said, waving an arm. "They trust me, but that's because they haven't any choice.

46

They've been bred for wool and meat and they couldn't lamb by theirselves if they wanted to; it's been bred out of them. But what they feel's only shallow; if Canker-lug was out lambing in the field and you didn't hold her down tight she'd be off and running. She's not bright enough to know it's for her own good. A horse is different." He stopped. "It's stupid telling you this."

"Honestly, I'd like to understand." Kitty sat, arms wrapped round her knees, watching him as he moved restlessly about, trying to describe something by waving his hands, or leaned back on the side of the pen.

"The trust a ewe feels when she's lambing isn't what I'd call a true trust because she's hiding her real nature till she sees a chance to give you the slip and bugger off. But a horse is a character in his own right. He's like you and me, he makes his own decision, deep down inside his self, and if he's broke right he trusts you enough to want to please you and do what you say. You can break a horse so you break his spirit, but then he'll be no good. There's a dealer I know breaks foals by tying them to a post with three halters – so they ain't got a chance of breaking free – then getting everyone he can lay hands on to bang pots, rev motorbikes, play stereos and all. By the end he reckons that foal won't move a muscle at a brass band. He's broke. He is and all. He ain't never going to trust anyone again but he won't run away because he's scared to. Now how I break a horse to noise is I'm good to him; I don't break his spirit. I get him halter-broke and we go out together, round the farm and up the roads, and if there's a car pissing about I just talks to him, calms him down, and then he knows that when I'm with him he's safe." He swallowed. "Now, that mare, when she was a filly she didn't want to go in the stable, she liked the fields. She didn't feel safe indoors, it wasn't natural to her to go in and sleep where she couldn't hear the night animals calling. But she went in because she wanted to please me, and she trusted me to be right when I said there weren't nothing to be afraid of. And then when I'm beside her you come falling out the sky like a punch in the mouth. When you did that you spoiled her. She can't forget. A piece of that trust's gone, and it won't never come back."

Kitty didn't know what to say; she couldn't believe that what she'd done was so irreparable. Hadn't she seen him calm the mare while she was in the stable? She didn't dare argue, though. She hung her head and stared at the floor.

"If you feel sorry you can help by staying away from Blossom. If you see her out in the fields you walk the other way; far as she's concerned you're poison." Jack tipped his hat over his eyes again and left the barn. He walked with a definite swagger, and despite his height, wore boots with heels.

Kitty watched the lamb as it searched for a drink with only the haziest idea of sheep anatomy. A tear dropped on the straw and she wiped her cheek. Stupid the way she always cried; tears with her were like a pressure valve, they escaped without her volition whenever a critical level of emotion was reached. What she felt now was a sense of injustice, and guilt, too, at having unwittingly harmed what Jack valued. Most of all she felt excluded, firmly set aside as being of no account compared to a horse, and it was this she resented to the point of tears.

She didn't want to go back to the house. She went out and leaned on a gate at the foot of the drive instead, staring up at the sun setting on the horizon and the blotches of gorse and scrub dripping down the sides of the valley. What was she doing here? She must be mad. She didn't belong. This was worse than working in a restaurant; at least there she'd known the rules. The wind blew on her face and a sheep nibbling at a chunk of dirt the other side of the gate came up to smell her shoe, and leapt back with exaggerated horror when she stretched out her hand. It was a disgustingly grimy sheep, bristling with brambles and clods of dung. Strange, too, that it was entirely on its own. She had a vague feeling that sheep liked to stroll around in gangs. As she was thinking this it charged into the hedge beside her and disappeared. There was a tremendous snapping of twigs and when Kitty investigated she saw the sheep was wedged tight, its face scarcely visible behind a mesh of thorns and bramble. It seemed quite content, champing on a twig, but she thought she'd better tell Roger or Jack. She could hear Roger shouting nearby.

"And you can forget the four pound because I'm never going to give it you." His voice was coming from the milking parlour. "What makes me think that? I'm not so mazed I don't know what I've lambed and what I haven't. Don't get me wrong. I'm pleased, shows you're not all bad. But if you want the work make your blooming mind up now, else I'll have to get a man in. I can't manage on me own." It was a surprise to Kitty, to hear Roger talking like this. His voice was bullying and hard, quite unlike the comical character she knew from the kitchen. There was a murmur in reply, and Roger continued. "I've better things to do than argue with you. If you're here when I come back I'll take it as settled." He crossed the yard to the barn. Kitty waited until he'd gone before coming out of hiding. Jack was leaning against the parlour doorway, arms folded.

"There's a sheep stuck in the hedge back there," she said. "I thought you ought to know."

"I seen her. There's no keeping her in; she's last year's pet lamb." He turned away.

"You're not giving in, are you?" Kitty asked, the words escaping before she had time to consider if they were wise.

"You can keep quiet and all," he growled. "I don't have to take stick from you."

49

4

"You ever hear about Norman and his unlucky week?"

The three men, Roger, Pug and Jack, were sitting round the kitchen table while Kitty washed up at the sink.

"I can't recall whether I have or no," Jack said unconvincingly.

"I has," said Roger, but not loud enough to put Pug off. Kitty rinsed the grapefruit glasses and began buffing them to a shine. Now Jack had capitulated over his wages he was allowed in the house for meals, and Pug had started calling again. Over the past ten days they'd had many long sessions like this, drinking coffee and talking. Pug would never eat anything Kitty had cooked; "There's a hot dinner waiting for me at home," he'd explain proudly to Roger, but she'd noticed that if she put out a plate of plain packet biscuits he'd occasionally snap one into bits and toss it in his mouth. Kitty sensed she should pretend she wasn't part of the social gathering, and make as little noise as possible, but it was obvious that much of what was said was aimed at her, like this story. Pug, who wouldn't look her in the eye, and only made sarcastic remarks about her to a third party – "Looks like your new house-keeper's making a proper job," he'd say to the others as she took a blackened sponge cake out of the oven – was nevertheless determined not to pass up the chance of a fresh audience for his anecdotes.

"It started on the Monday. Norman went to have a talk with Mr Haskins up at the Hall, walked in the gun room and found him dead. Like a slaughterhouse, it were; he'd shot his self with his rifle. The coppers said he hadn't been too careful when he were cleaning his gun, or else he'd had a private trouble they didn't know of. That's what they said, but they was hard men: seemed like they reckoned Norman might have had a deal to do with it. He said after that he never wanted to see another copper as long as he lived."

"Wednesday," he went on, snapping a biscuit. "He was out early checking his hen pheasants when he sees a car where it didn't ought to be, up Green Lane, engine running and all. He thought at first it were a courting couple, till he got up close and saw it were a grockle in a business suit what had gassed his self with a length of rubber tubing. Norman stared at that there telephone up by the shop a good half hour before he found it in him to ring the coppers. And didn't they give him some stick? Reckoned they had one of they mass murderers on their hands." He gave a yap of laughter and tossed a piece of biscuit in his mouth.

Kitty glanced sideways at the three men. Roger was hunched, head down, thinking hard about some problem, not listening to the story at all. Jack was tipped back in his chair, arms folded behind his head, smiling at Pug. He hadn't talked to Kitty since the lambing incident. At mealtimes Roger would come in first and sit down to take off his boots; a pointless exercise because by then he'd already tracked mud across half the floor. While he was unknotting his laces with frankfurter fingers Jack could be heard in the dog's room, whispering excitedly:

"Rats! Where are they? Hey? Bite them. Go on then, boy!"

Roger would shout crossly, "Don't fuss the dog: your food's ready and waiting," and Jack would pad in in his socks, his hands flushed from the yard tap, and eat fast and silently, never raising his head. When he'd finished he'd nod at his father and go back outside; unlike Roger he never had a dessert or a sugary cup of tea. But when Pug was there they behaved quite differently. All three of them would walk in together, talking and laughing, and Jack would relax in his chair and smile, though not at Kitty. He never acknowledged her presence, except by dipping his head lower when she sat down to eat at table.

From her point of social invisibility she'd noticed how sharply Pug's glittering eyes sized up the others' moods; now, judging he'd paused long enough, he finished his story.

"After that you couldn't get Norman out of his house without a struggle. You should have seen him: jittery, hands trembling; he could hardly lift a pint to his lips without spilling it. Well, he got through the rest of the week without any bother, and on the Sunday he made up his mind to go to church, not that he was a religious man, but to set things right with his maker. And he was just coming up the rise to the churchyard when one of they light aircraft crashes bang! into the electric pylon in front of him."

There was a pause, broken by soot tinkling down the stove ventilator.

"Wind's changing," said Roger. "Best if we gets the rest of those sheep off the hills. Dog'll do it."

"He's too fat," said Jack, winking at Pug.

"There's fat and there's fit, and he's fit."

"How can he be fit? Only time he takes any exercise is when he opens his mouth to eat more of my layer's mash."

"Your layer's mash? Who pays the bill?"

"I'll pay you back when I gets my wages."

Roger got disgustedly to his feet and whistled. Claws scrabbled on concrete in the next room, and something flopped. Then there was silence.

"Call that fit?" Jack called out.

"He's more use than some I could mention. Least he does what he's told." They heard Roger patting the dog, then his command "Here, Fly."

Pug crammed his tweed cap on his head and muttered, "No rest for the wicked," adding to Jack as Roger's shadow fell across the kitchen window: "You coming up tonight?"

"He'd never let me."

"You don't need his say so."

"I've to mind the ewes."

"They can spare you half an hour, can't they?" Pug put his arm round Jack's shoulders. "Don't let him put you down: you'll never get out from under."

"It's already happened, hasn't it?"

"It don't have to be like that."

Kitty, watching them walk out into the yard, hoped Jack wouldn't give in to Pug's coaxing. She knew it was unfair, but she distrusted Pug, because she disliked his face. It looked worse today, shiny and inflamed, like a ball of pink wax.

When they'd gone she went listlessly upstairs with the Hoover. The sexy calendar in the hall had comments scribbled on it at random intervals: "Polly due", "1178 on heat". The day of her arrival a spiky hand had put "fresh chicken!", and tomorrow, the first of March, had "1.G" written across it. She felt this might mean a new guest arriving, so she opened the window in the last empty bedroom to air it. The mattress had a calico cover, and folded neatly on top were a collection of blankets, each with about three different things wrong with it – a rusty stain, an obsessive darn and a moth hole, say – strategically placed so there was only one possible way of putting the blanket on to prevent its flaws being immediately obvious. It was like a Chinese puzzle, Kitty thought, ripping off the top blanket and substituting another to conceal what resembled a gigantic fossilised bird-dropping, hammered flat and varnished. This wasn't a pleasant room. It overlooked a largish lake the Snells had constructed and filled, for a reason Kitty found hard to fathom, with liquid animal manure. Banks of unappetising froth were floating busily about on its surface, and overhanging it was a metallic building painted brilliant lime. The same decorator, with an instinct for instilling gloom and nausea, had papered this room with hairy purple flock. There wasn't a bedspread. Kitty pulled out the empty drawers in the wardrobe, searching for one, but all she came across were dried woodlice and yellowed newspaper. The bed didn't look complete without a flounced nylon cover, now she'd got her eye in for the Snell style of interior decoration. Surely there must be one, in a violently unsuitable colour like diarrhoea brown or electric blue? It couldn't be in any of the cupboards downstairs, she'd already looked through them, but maybe it was in Roger's room.

The pale green fibres of Roger's bedroom carpet still stood on end after yesterday's hoovering; there was a dark channel from the door to the bed where his feet had ruffled them. His bedclothes had been hurled about in a frenzy and one slipper was balanced on top of the narrow chest of drawers beside the window. Amused by how energetic he was in his sleep, Kitty went over and looked through the drawers. Those at the top were full of clothes – nylon roll-neck sweaters in dusty black, 'indestructible' socks that had gone crisp in the tumble-drier, tired long johns and quantities of mildewed beige trousers – but there was only a striped bolster in the bottom one. She pulled the drawer out a little further, to see if there was a bedspread at the back, and it dropped on the floor with a bang. A soft fluttering noise followed, and two letters drifted down from the lining of the chest. They were folded up, and written on thin blue airmail paper, but even before she'd completely unwrapped them Kitty knew they'd been written by Deborah May. There was no mistaking her neat copperplate.

Dear Hilda,

I was sorry not to see you at the wedding, but I know it was too far for you to travel. Your dishes are very welcome, the van brought them Friday last.

It was a good clear day for the wedding and Dad said I had never looked finer. Rog's half of the church was not full, but I never cared for his family and do not mind if they are not agreeable. It was queer marrying him after all the trouble. He did not look happy and I was grieved for him. I do hope to be a good wife and make up to him for all I have done wrong.

He is kind to me, but I feel awkward in his house, and there is old Mrs S. to watch out for. Rog says I am to work outside and leave the indoors to her but I do not think I can stick her housekeeping!

There are docks and horse dashiels all over and no hard standings, and it will be a long job to get the farm up together. It is queer getting used to Rog's ways. He is so different from Dad, not just in the farming, but slow and shy. Before, he was always so cocky, but that was because he was with Philip. Philip left when it all came out about the baby and no one has seen him since. It is better that way, if he was here I would never settle. Old Mrs S. says we will miss him at hay making.

Please write soon and send all the news,

Your loving

Deb.

Kitty unfolded the second letter. Like the first, it had been handled so frequently that the edges felt furry. Deborah May's writing fluctuated a great deal. At the beginnings and ends of her letters it was upright and precise, but whenever she wrote about Roger it sloped, and the words squashed up and became difficult to read.

Dear Hilda,

I am writing to tell you that you have a godson, born Sunday. I am calling him Jack after Great Uncle Jack. You do not have to watch his spiritual welfare, the vicar will do that, but mind you send him plenty of presents!

We were turning the hay Saturday, and it was too wet for baling, but Rog said there was rain coming and we had to get it in the barn. I said the clouds were wrong for rain, but he said he knew best and I talked too much.

I never want to see bales like that again. It was like carrying stones, and the worst of it was, I was afraid of harming the baby. I could feel the pulling inside when I lifted. When it was all in and stacked the sun came out. You will never guess what Rog did then. I never saw the like in all the years with Dad. He only made me take it all out again, cut the strings and set it to dry. Then my labour started and I was spared further work, and it was fine hay at the finish. But what a carry on!

I do not mean to tell tales, but I can not seem to help it, and you are the only one I can tell them to. I want to feel for him the way I did, but that was spoilt last year, I can not make it come back. It would be better if we were the kind to talk, but he will never listen. I do like him, and respect him, but I always have the other in my mind.

Jack is eight pound and handsome, and I had an

easy labour. If I knew where Philip was living I would send him the news. Do not worry, I am a good girl now.

I wish you would write.

Many kisses from me and Jack,

Your loving

Deb.

There were no more letters, though Kitty pulled all the drawers out and felt along the backs. She longed to read more, she was beginning to feel starved of print. There weren't any books at Balls Farm, except for her copy of *The History of Western Philosophy*, which she carried everywhere, in the hope that desperation would force her to read it. There was a consolation prize for all her searching, though: squashed under the bolster was a nylon gauze bedspread, as frilly as a sexy nightdress, with a large hole in the middle, as if some guest, frustrated beyond endurance, had snapped at it.

After reading the letters Kitty felt restless, and when evening came and she'd finished her work, she went outside. She couldn't take a proper walk; she was frightened to go too far in any direction in case she got lost in the dark, but each day she felt a stronger urge to explore her surroundings, and each day, too, the house seemed stuffier and more oppressive. Miss Biffen was knitting in front of the television, Mrs Ridley staring at it with stiff disapproval, as if she expected it to make a rude noise. Kitty watched them through the window. She loved observing people secretly, like a ghost. As she gazed into the snug, brightly lit room, her nose cold on the window pane, she tried to imagine what it would be like if she actually was a ghost, and deeply attached to either of the two ladies; how sad it would be to have to watch them and be forever shut off from contact. She'd have to be a ghost romantically attached to Miss Biffen, she decided. Mayonne Ridley was too prickly for anyone to love. Miss Biffen had taken her aside this evening.

"Kitty, dear," she'd said, "you mustn't mind Mayonne. She's really very happy here and she doesn't mean half of what she says." (Mayonne had found dog hairs in the butter and given Kitty a stinging lecture on hygiene. Kitty was mystified; apart from her first day, she'd never seen the dog move. Had it learnt how to open the refrigerator and scramble into the butter-dish? Did it drop into the dining room via the chimney?) "She can be a dear person, but she doesn't take easily to new faces. Why, we have such happy evenings together." Was this a happy evening? The two ladies were sitting well apart, not talking or looking at each other, their faces lit by the luminous flicker of the television. "She's had a sad life." Miss Biffen had frowned so that powder compacted in ridges on her forehead. "She lost her husband ten years ago. I've never seen anyone so inconsolable, she could barely speak for months. I was only an acquaintance then, and it was her grief that brought us together. It broke my heart to see her in pain. She has such dignity. I'm afraid I've never been like that: Silly Gilly, that's me."

"How did he die?"

Miss Biffen lowered her voice. "He had a heart attack, it was very awkward for her – the circumstances." Kitty didn't ask any more questions, she simply tried to look kind and not particularly interested as she cleared and dusted the dining room, and eventually Miss Biffen confided that he'd died on the lavatory. It was ironic that Mayonne of all people should have been singled out to bear such an indecorous tragedy. Kitty half wanted to laugh at the cruel ridiculousness of it, but she couldn't help feeling sympathy too. Perhaps there was courage and strength in that hard, whiskery face. Mayonne suddenly got up and came over to the window, and Kitty, secure in the knowledge that she was completely invisible, didn't flinch. The old lady fiddled with the window-catch. She must be too hot, not surprising considering the number of heaters going in there.

"Will you go away and stop staring at me? Didn't your mother ever tell you it was rude?" Mrs Ridley poked her face through the tiny window and Kitty ran off, blushing with shame, and didn't stop until she was at the door of the barn.

She peered in. The sheep were hushed. One bare electric light swung from the roof, twirling in the eddies of wind from the open door. Everywhere she looked Kitty could see ewes lying down; they favoured a sideways position, stomachs bulged out over the straw. Most were chewing the cud; every so often there'd be a cough or a rustle as an uncomfortably fat stomach was rearranged. Jack was at the far end, shaking a bale of straw, his back to her. She wouldn't stay long, she'd just have a brief look at the animals and be gone. She wandered up the rows of pens, finding herself drawn to the one she'd noticed last time she was here, where the lamb she'd found in the kitchen was kept under a low lamp. He was still there, trembling and silent, his back bent in a hoop, like a cat in the attack position. His face, small and bony, reminded her of Lance. Maybe she'd call him Lancelot. She sat down and touched him with her fingers and he twirled his tail and began wailing.

"Now you've wound him up good and proper you can feed him," Jack called.

Kitty was surprised he was speaking to her again. "What with?"

"Milk. It's down by the side."

She searched unsuccessfully while the lamb's cries became shriller. Sheep, disturbed by the noise, began getting to their feet and baaing back, and lambs appeared from everywhere – under hay, behind buckets, the folds of their mother's wool – and blared their sympathy. It was like the climactic number in a farmyard musical, and as it reached fever pitch Jack swore loudly. Kitty recoiled as he approached, expecting another tirade, perhaps on how she'd permanently damaged the lamb's emotional health by touching him lightly on the head. She didn't get it. Jack produced a sack of white powder and a bottle and jug and explained how to mix a drink for a lamb. She felt annoyed by his rudeness, but kept quiet. It was only in exceptional circumstances that she ever found the courage to stand up for herself. It was easier and more effective to accept abuse with dignity. The articles on assertiveness she'd read, hoping to improve herself, had never mentioned the chastening effect this tactic often had, even on a hardened bully, when answering back or being tearfully aggrieved would only have provoked. Besides, Jack was drunk.

Alcohol billowed out of him, masking his usual sweet smell. Kitty had noticed at their first meeting that he was one of those lucky people whose skin gives out a natural flowery perfume. She'd always been acutely aware of smells. Such queasy sharpness of perception went with being a migraine personality. To her each human being sat in the centre of a funnel of odour, three or four feet at its widest, the edges wobbling as they battled with other perfumes. Roger, for instance, smelt of vinegar in the evenings, when he relaxed in the lounge, and treacly and powdery from animal cake in the morning. Miss Biffen had one of those strong, fleshy smells, like raw pork, that timid people often have, as if it were the only way of impressing their personality on their surroundings. And Mrs Ridley emanated dry-cleaning fluid, especially from her mouth, a sure sign she didn't soak her plate properly; dirty dentures smelt quite different from dirty teeth. Smell had been the worst aspect of living in London, particularly the sickly bath of blended deodorant Kitty had had to submerge herself in each morning as she boarded a crowded tube train. She'd been surprised to find the country wasn't much better; the land round the Snell farm gave off vividly intimate odours, reminiscent of socks left mouldering at the bottom of a laundry basket and ancient cheesy underpants.

Jack pressed a full bottle of milk into her hand. "Here," he said, the irritation gone from his voice, although the sheep had reached a further crescendo of baaing. "He's hungry, that's why he's making such a pissing awful noise. Me and the old man never get round to feeding him."

He lifted the lamb out and settled him in Kitty's lap, then showed her how to ease the chipolata-shaped teat into his mouth. Lancelot whimpered in protest, but soon settled to a steady sucking, and Jack sat beside Kitty and adjusted the bottle a millimetre; drink made him extra meticulous rather than unsteady.

"Careful," he said. "Don't let him take in air, because a sheep can't fart. Makes them better company than humans. There's a lot of nasty habits animals miss out on: like a horse can't urge to save his life."

"Urge?"

"Throw up, be sick."

"Can a horse get drunk?" Kitty asked cheekily

"He can get drunk on oats. They'll go straight to his head and make him wild. Even old oats'll do that, and you have to work them out of him; set him in a plough and work him till he's sober. But new oats! When Blossom was three year old I gave her some of the old man's oats before Christmas. They've a poison in them until the old year's out, but I didn't know that then, I just wanted to give her a sparkle. So I took some of his oats from the bin and she went mad. She was screaming and spinning round in her stall. Evil. I didn't know what to do, so I goes and tells Pug and he puts me on her back, opens the stable door and tells me to ride it out of her. Did she gallop? I'll never forget that ride.

Three hours I was on her back; she went up the valley and into the trees, across five farms, and she kept going till she reached the sea. I was only thirteen then, and holding tight to her mane, didn't have no tack or nothing, and she was screaming as she went."

"Was she all right?"

"She was dripping wet come the finish, and her stomach sounded like the pub at chucking-out time, but she got over it. We didn't get home till half-way through next morning; that was another day I missed school." He smiled at her, pink skin crinkling at the corners of his mouth, so he resembled a laughing piglet in a child's cartoon, then put out a finger and traced one of the plucked eyebrows. "Why'd you take them away?" he murmured. "I liked them."

She looked down at the lamb, suddenly shy. Lancelot had finished all his milk and fallen asleep. "Why'd you come here?" Jack asked. "You're not like the others."

"What others?"

"The other housekeepers."

Kitty was shocked. Despite the fact that Roger had mentioned a previous housekeeper, she'd somehow assumed that she was the first. "How many have there been?"

"More than you could keep a count of."

"What about . . . Kitty hesitated. "What about your mother?"

"Oh she cleared off years ago. I was still at school when she went. I come home one afternoon and she'd gone. Didn't leave a letter or nothing. The old man said she give him a piece of her mind and caught the bus." Jack stroked the lamb's head. "I don't blame her, he's ignorant."

"What do you mean? Stupid?"

"No. Ignorant. Like he don't think of anyone but his self. I used to hear them arguing. She'd say she was leaving and he'd say, 'Go on, then, leave. You know where the door is. I can soon get another maid to wash my shirts.' She didn't want to, then." He took his hand away from the lamb and it twitched an ear. "You're clever, you are." He said. "You keep getting me to gab on about me self but you haven't answered my question. Why'd you come here?"

"I wanted to escape, I suppose. To people who live in towns the countryside seems ideal, like a dream: just animals and fresh air, and people behaving instinctively. Being more honest with each other. Of course I know it's not like that now, but that's why I wanted to come. And now I suppose . . . " her voice trailed off, "I suppose I like some bits of it for quite different reasons. I like the way the sheep are so – difficult. I didn't know animals were like that: so determined and grumpy."

"What about the old man? Do you like him?"

"I don't dislike him. He's nice to me. I don't think he's very kind to you, but he's different when you're not there. A bit ridiculous, harmless."

Jack grinned. "That's one thing he's not. You watch out, he'll jump anything. Grab a granny, he would. That's why the housekeepers don't last long."

"You mean he . . . "

"Course he does. It's easier than going out and looking for it, isn't it?"

"Oh no, I'm sure you're wrong," said Kitty, aghast." I don't think he . . . I'm sure he doesn't fancy me. I don't think he's even looked at me."

"He don't. That's not his way. He thinks about it for a few weeks, and then he does it, a bit sudden."

"What exactly does he do?" Kitty put the bottle down.

"Don't ask me. He's not going to do it when I'm there, is he? All I know is there's all this screaming from the house in the middle of the night and next day the housekeeper's packed her bags and gone. Of course some likes it and stays."

"You're joking?" Kitty pleaded, but Jack shook his head and laughed.

"I'm not, honest. Would I tell a lie? I'm pissed out of me tree, and I never lie when I'm pissed." He pulled a half-empty bottle of whisky out of his pocket. "Do you want some?"

Kitty disapproved. Wasn't he supposed to be minding the sheep? He wouldn't be able to if he got much drunker.

"I'm celebrating," he said. "The end of a horse. The end of a line of horses. It couldn't have happened to a finer." He drank, whisky trickling down his chin.

"What horse? One of yours?"

"No. One I wanted, and couldn't have. I saw him at Christmas, when I was delivering a goose to a scrapyard on the coast. He's a real hard case, Eli, what runs the yard. This bloke come once, one of these vintage car plonkers, looking for a windscreen to finish off a Lanchester he had, that he'd been doing up for the last ten years. You can't get that kind of stuff any more, there's none left, not the genuine article. Eli had one out the back and he says it's ten quid, and this plonker gets out his wallet and starts in with 'I'm frightfully sorry but I've only got five pounds on me, will that do,' meaning to bargain. You can't play games with Eli. That windscreen must have been worth well over fifty quid, if it wasn't priceless, and Eli knew it, so he says, 'I'll show you what you can do with your five pound,' and he picks the glass up and smashes it on his knee."

The lamb had fallen asleep. Its head was resting warmly on Kitty's arm, and she could feel its pulse beating: a fast, breathless patter. Its skin had the sweet, fatty odour of roast lamb; she hadn't realised before that animals smelt the same cooked as alive.

"He's rolling in it, Eli," Jack went on. "That's where the money is, in scrap. There's times I look round at this farm and think what an ace scrapyard it'd make." He turned the bottle thoughtfully in his hand. "Eli wasn't in when I got there. His dog was chained and howling, and I thought I'd have a sniff round for an axle. There's a couple of old pig huts up by the beach where he stores bits out the wet. And that's where I saw the horse." Kitty could tell Jack was getting agitated; he began to rub the side of his face with his palm, and push his fingers through his hair, slow actions that he repeated over and over, as if to soothe himself. "He were cramped in one of them huts, it fitted him so tight he couldn't hardly raise his head, and the hay with him was black. Dusty and mouldy? You wouldn't bed cattle with it.

"I never seen a carthorse like that before. An entire, a strawberry roan with a grey mane and tail, but it was the shape of him hit you in the eye. He hadn't been fed decent, but you could see he was made solid: big springy ribs, and a good deep chest on him. His legs was like this," Jack stuck his arms stiffly out in front of him, and clenched his fists, so his forearms bulged. "The muscle on that stallion! And he was poor, you could see he was poor, his eyes was sunk right back in his head, and his coat greasy and crawling with lice. But he had a good eye, kind and soft.

"Eli come back then, and caught me looking. He said he were a French horse, a new breed to this country, an Ardennes (Jack pronounced it Ar-deans), what he was fattening up for the meat trade. I didn't have no money, I never got no pissing money, but I had a deal with him, beat him down from what he wanted, and he said I could have the stallion, long as I give him eight hundred pound before the first of March."

Jack picked up Kitty's hand and turned it so he could see her gold watch. She tensed; she wasn't sure she liked him touching her so frequently, but he only wanted to see what time it was. "See," he said, "I've only an hour to find the money. I reckon I've lost that stallion."

"He's still there?"

"Oh yes. Thinner. He's much thinner. He's losing condition all the time. The pity of it is he's so much growing to do, and if he don't do it now he'll never catch up, always be stunted. He can't do without the right grub. Eli's got him good hay now, but that's not enough for a growing stallion; Eli don't know shit about horses, and it's no use telling him, he'd just turn nasty. I can't stand to see that blood-line wasted, neither. See, heavy horses all but died out fifty year ago, and people was only keeping them for shows. You want different qualities for working: show stallions are too big and evil-tempered. We ain't got the right stock now in England to breed good workers, but that French stallion could sire handsome foals. He's got everything: strength and a quiet nature. I've never seen his equal." Jack sighed and lifted the whisky bottle; his face was rosy from drink, the edges of his lips blurred.

"Couldn't you raise the money?"

"If the old man had made it four quid I could have, easy, but there's no chance now."

Kitty could hear a pulse beating in her head. It was always like that when she was about to make a rash decision: like standing on an underground platform as the train approached, half-scared, half exhilarated, noise ringing in her ears and the world about to fragment around her. "How much did you raise?"

"Five hundred-odd. I sold Blossom's yearling. But it's not enough."

Kitty swallowed. "I could lend you the rest."

"No. Forget it. It's just the way things are. I don't expect to have everything I want; and if I bought the horse he'd just as likely drop dead the next day."

"But I could. Your dad owes me nearly three weeks' wages and there's this gold watch. I think it's quite valuable."

Jack shook his head.

"You could give me a share in him, like people do with racehorses, and buy me out later," Kitty pleaded, tearful at the thought of the poor stallion shrivelling up in his tight-fitting hut. Besides, this was a chance for her to make up for hurting Blossom.

"It'd be wrong of me to do it, take money from you," Jack said slowly. He smiled suddenly. "Bloody tempting, though."

"Well, why don't you? I'll go and get the money off your dad."

"He'll be asleep."

"Then I'll just have to wake him up."

5

It was a strange sensation riding in a cart. Kitty had never been in one before, and she'd vaguely imagined it would be like those closed carriages heroines stepped out of in historical dramas. It wasn't. It was an open box made from loose nails and splintery wood, and far colder than she would ever have believed possible: an unbeatable frostbite combination of staying in one position while icy winds played on you from unexpected directions. She was sitting down, but you couldn't exactly say she wasn't moving: the cart struck her incessantly on the bum from below, and sometimes hurled her violently from side to side. It didn't seem to affect Jack the same way: he was standing steadily at the front like a charioteer, holding the reins while Blossom trotted with a rhythmic jingle of chain. The harness creaked like a gigantic leather coat being crumpled and released, and every so often Blossom would release a low, murmuring fart. It was a pity horses *could* fart. What a shame it wasn't the other way round and sheep were the ones who couldn't be sick. She was sure a sheep's wind wouldn't be as intolerably fruity as Blossom's, and anyway you were never forced to sit behind a sheep for long periods.

"Ho!" Jack called, and Blossom slowed. "Easy now. Take it steady." They were going down a steep slope, and Blossom began to walk with a fat-bottomed, mincing gait, her body the only brake on the cart careering down the rutted, overgrown lane ahead of them. She slid, stiff-legged, on the mud, and Jack leapt down and walked beside her, holding her bridle in his fist and muttering encouragement, their heads close together. Kitty could hear the sea rolling pebbles as the cart twisted past a thicket of trees and stopped, sheets of damp cardboard and torn newspaper clinging to the wheels. Ahead of her was a crazily dirty landscape. The moon was waxing, only a thin crescent, but it glimmered off the bumpers of a thousand cars, and the horizon was blotted out by a towering slag heap of discarded tyres. In the centre was a small hut, light streaming from its open door, a dog's silhouette leaping and falling at the end of a rope.

"You made it, then?" A man had appeared beside the cart. He was as tall as Jack, but much wider, with pale hair and loose, rumpled skin on his face. He smiled when he saw Kitty, as if he'd just heard the punch line of a subtle joke, and she saw the flash of a metal tooth. There was something shamefaced about the way Jack asked: "That Ardeans stallion ain't gone on to the knackers yet?"

Eli winked at him and said: "No, no, I'd have waited till the morning. You've saved me a journey and done the horse a favour." He helped Kitty courteously down from the cart. "You'll take a drink?"

She declined: she wanted to be alone. Everything had happened too fast. She hadn't had time to think seriously about what she was doing until just now, when the cart ride had dampened her frenzy of self-sacrifice. It hadn't been difficult to get the money out of Roger. He'd acted as if it was quite normal for employees to shake their bosses awake in the middle of the night and demand their wages instantly, in cash.

"I don't know why I has maids for housekeepers," he'd said, climbing mildly out of his bed in stained long johns, and showing no trace of his fabled lechery. "They always gets so fired up; get some idea in their daft heads and they can't wait to act on it." He'd opened a drawer in his frilled dressing table. Inside were a pair of wire spectacles – which he'd unfolded and fitted slowly on his nose – some ledgers and a roll of money. He'd glanced at her over the top of the glasses like a benign old uncle. "Now don't you go telling Jack where this cash is, or it'll be gone; runs through it like whisky, he do." He'd written in a ledger with surprisingly even, well-educated handwriting while Kitty fidgeted with impatience, aware that the minutes were trickling away. "Now if you'll sign your name there," he'd said, "saying as how you've had the cash, we can be all square. I been caught like that before." He'd finished by clicking his tongue as he counted out the notes and grumbling: "I don't know, I do think you've got the better of me. It's a dear business, paying housekeepers. It grieves me to see it go."

The pounds rustled in her pocket. She could hear Jack and Eli laughing in the distance. There was so much she could do with this money if she kept it. It was her freedom. She could go abroad as she'd planned – well, when she'd earned a bit more – or she could buy an outfit so irresistible it would melt Lance's stony heart and make him fall in love with her. She winced. What was really going to hurt, so much that she didn't want to think about it, was parting with his watch. She knew he hadn't wanted her to have it. On her birthday she'd tearfully accused him of never giving her anything, not even a keepsake, and with sarcastic bad grace he'd taken off his antique gold watch and presented it to her. She'd felt ashamed for the rest of the day. Now the fat, red-gold links glittered under her sleeve, hanging on her wrist as if they knew it was the last time too and were reluctant to let go. She mustn't think like that; the horse was a living, suffering creature, and far more important than any jewellery. She climbed out of the cart and walked towards the corrugated hut she could see half-hidden in the trees, wanting to see the stallion before she committed herself.

The door creaked as she pulled it, and she tensed: she didn't want the men to know she was here. She wanted to make her decision privately. It was stuffy inside, so dark she felt blind, and she could hear a whiffling noise. Something soft and moist touched her forehead and mumbled at it, like the tip of an elephant's trunk. She stood perfectly still and the soft, rubbery thing went higher and sampled her hair with infinite gentleness, separating the strands and tasting them before retreating into the darkness. She put up her hand and touched bony flesh beneath coarse fur. It trembled but didn't withdraw; invisibly alert. She couldn't see the horse, so she couldn't be frightened by him; she could only sense his character, his massive power. Something quite complex was living in that shed, not broken and pitiful, as she'd expected, but only saddened by experience. She moved her hand away from the horse's face and he leaned forward to make contact again, brushing his lips delicately against her wrist, as if he knew she was wary and was determined not to alarm her.

"You can have the watch," she whispered. "I couldn't leave you here."

When she saw the stallion in the moonlight Kitty was horrified. He shivered in the wind off the sea, enormously broad, his ribs like the hoops of a barrel, the flesh below them sucked in by starvation, and his shabby, whiskery hair worn away in patches. When she patted him lice fled from her hand. Inside, in the dark, she'd visualised a body heaving with muscle; this animal looked more like a famished donkey than a horse. He paced slowly along behind the cart, at the end of a halter, head low, eyes half-shut. Now there was no deadline Blossom could amble instead of trot, and Jack balanced on the side of the cart, reins held loosely in one hand, studying his new purchase.

"He doesn't seem very happy to be free," she observed.

Jack didn't respond at first, then he muttered: "He's tired."

Hedges scratched against the sides of the cart; Kitty was so high up she could see over the tops into meadows where sheep lay sleeping, pale and flat as giant mushrooms. One field was full of metal pens. There was a terrified grunt from the nearest as the cart jingled past, and a sow bolted from the opening and raced down the side of the hedge, ten pale blobs pursuing her and squealing with distress.

"Your dad keeps pigs, doesn't he?" Kitty asked.

Jack nodded, glancing from one horse to the other.

"Why doesn't he keep them out in a field, like these?" All Kitty knew about the Snell pigs was that they lived in a long blockhouse and frequently tussled inside it. You could hear heavy bodies thudding onto concrete, and the odd snort of hatred and irritation. She'd never seen them, only smelt them extremely strongly.

"He fattens them, he don't breed them," Jack said, after a pause.

"What difference does that make?"

"Think about it."

Kitty was angry. What right had he to be so curt when she'd just given him all her money and valuables? Surely he ought to put himself out more considering how much he owed her? She tried to think of a suitably rude remark, but none came, so she turned her head stiffly away from him to indicate her displeasure.

"If you want to get fat you sit still and stuff your face, don't you?" Jack said suddenly. "They'd need more feed if they was out." He didn't sound hostile, just tired and reflective, like the stallion.

72

"Don't they get bored indoors?" Kitty ventured, feeling like a child with a weary adult for company.

Jack raised his voice and called, "Wog off, Blossom," and the mare veered right at a crossroads.

"Wog off?" Kitty giggled. "What kind of an order is that? Why don't you just say 'turn right'?"

"Don't ask me. There's no reason for it. It's just horseman's language. 'Wog off' is right, and 'come here' left." He jingled the reins and Blossom speeded up briefly before reverting to her usual plump, swaying step, like a fat woman in high heels.

It was cruel to force Jack to talk when he didn't feel like it. Kitty watched the stars instead. The cold and the darkness made her wistful, and she found herself thinking about all she'd lost and would maybe never see again. Her wrist felt strange without the gold watch, lighter and colder, and Lance himself seemed even more remote, now all tangible proof of their relationship was gone.

She'd loved him the moment she first saw him. He had a delicately boned head and brown hair so pale it was ash-coloured, and in the interview room, with the afternoon light dimming outside the window, he'd looked like a fine pencil drawing, the moustache and stubble on his chin closer to shading than hair. She'd had no way of knowing then that he was the most sought-after member of staff in the whole university, the campus equivalent of a rock star. She'd noticed how beautiful his clothes were, but their choice didn't look contrived; she'd assumed it was only by accident that they distilled the very essence of fashion.

There was a point in that interview when she'd been tempted to lie. Lance had inquired if she'd read two or three books, all classics which she should have been familiar with, and she'd had to say no. Then he'd asked her about George Eliot's *Middlemarch*.

"Yes, I have read it," she'd said, before instinct

73

prompted her to qualify this to "but only the first few chapters. I think she's a wonderful writer and I've read all her other books, but I just couldn't continue with that one."

"Why not?" Lance had leaned forward for the first time. His hands were folded in front of him and she'd seen his fingernails gleam.

"I liked the heroine, and I felt she was making the wrong decision. I could see she was going to marry that Casaubon, and I hated him, so I couldn't bear to read on. I do find it very hard to read painful scenes in novels. I don't see why art has to be so uncomfortable. Take anything – a radio play about a group of people climbing a mountain, for instance. Why isn't it interesting enough for them to just get on and climb it? Almost any writer, given that plot, will make one character deeply disagreeable and selfish, so they can goad all the other more sympathetic characters. It's so true of all literature, isn't it? Think of any great classic, even the Bible, and the central theme is always the pointless torture of a peaceable, hard-working individual."

"You don't think writers are trying to be true to life?"

"As far as I can see most lives aren't like that. Mine certainly isn't."

Perhaps he saw it as a challenge: the chance to play God and temper a calm, unworried soul with pain. Kitty was offered a place at the university, and put in Lance Billow's tutorial. He had a ridiculous name, but she'd noticed before that prominent people often did have peculiar names. His was especially apt: he seemed to favour big blonde girls, pink and gold, the colour of clouds at sunset, and the name conjured up a picture of him leaping on them energetically. He didn't seem energetic in tutorials – he was watchful and contained then, like a lizard stalking a fly.

"You're so bland," he accused once, after she'd digressed from discussing a book into explaining how easy it was to be happy. Just a matter of being warm and well fed and in the company of friends. Anyone could do it, she couldn't see why there was such anguish over it. "Can't you even imagine a state of mind where feelings have a sharper focus than your own?"

She'd tried very hard to please: spent hours in the library doing background reading and working on her essays. One afternoon her tutorial partner didn't arrive. He was often late, a grimy man who brought Marxism into every argument, and Lance was tapping his fingers on Kitty's work and staring past her head.

"You never give me what I ask for," he'd said suddenly. "The potential's there, but it's as if you can't make the leap into thought. Tell me, how total is your inexperience? Have you ever had a lover?"

She couldn't reply, but he must have guessed the answer because his behaviour altered: he'd torn her essay fastidiously in half and taken her by the hand. She could still remember the way she'd shivered as she felt that first contact. He'd led her along the deserted concrete walkways of the university, his full-skirted coat flapping behind him. The lights were just coming on, glowing orange against the smoky blue sky, and she remembered how she'd felt anxious that someone might see them holding hands and misinterpret it.

He'd stopped at the shop by the traffic-lights and bought a bottle of wine, releasing her so she trembled, her clothes too thin to keep out the cold.

"Never mind, you'll be warm soon," he'd said, and smiled at her, and she'd begun to feel so excited that she didn't notice where they went to after that. As far as she was concerned they were walking down the same endless concrete path, enclosed by bands of dark sky. She'd blinked with astonishment when she'd found herself outside her own college room, and it wasn't until later that she'd felt at all surprised that he'd known where she lived.

Inside it had smelt as usual of furniture spray and warm, brand new carpet. She'd felt ashamed of all her decorations: the poster that read "Today is the first day of the rest of your life", the postcard of the two cats curled up in a saucepan, and the other one of George Eliot. She'd always loved that picture, it touched her to the heart, the ludicrously ugly face with the huge nose like a beak, which vain efforts had been made to prettify with braided hair and lace. The eyes knew it was hopeless, they captured all the torment of looking like that in an unkind world.

"Have you ever had a drink before?" Lance had asked, unscrewing the cap.

"Of course I have. I'm not a baby!" Kitty had said indignantly. "You've got this funny idea of me as a total idiot that's done nothing and talks a load of rubbish, but where I come from everyone's like me. It's you that's different, your ideas that seem crazy to me."

"What have you done, then? Tell me," he'd asked, filling her coffee mug to the brim and passing it to her.

"You always do that," she'd replied sadly, taking a big gulp to show her sophistication and wincing at the bitter taste. "Turn everything round to make me look ridiculous. Of course it doesn't sound much, what I've done, but I am quite grown-up. I'm a hard worker, and I can look after myself. And you may think what I write is no good, but none of my other tutors do. At Middle English they're pleased with me."

"I bet they are," he'd said, drinking from the bottle. "I bet you're early for those 9.15 seminars and you've done all your homework, and you're full of lively ideas about Sir Gawain and the Green Knight. They've probably never come across such enthusiasm, such thorough determination to buckle down to work and do a good job."

"That's right," she'd said, nodding her head and then feeling foolish as she sensed the sarcasm behind his words.

He'd laughed. "I never look at you without thinking how much you're going to change in the next three years," he'd said. "I give those neat skirts and tights another six months at the most, and I don't somehow think that handknitted jersey's going to make it past the Christmas vac."

"Is that what you came here for, to laugh at me?"

"No." Lance had studied her with his faded blue eyes. "What do you think I came here for?" Her heart had moved painfully with excitement.

"Come here." He hadn't allowed her to sit primly beside him on the bed; he'd made her take a big mouthful of wine and then, when she was still recovering from swallowing it, kissed her.

"This is highly illegal," he'd said, when they were lying close together on the cover, and she was gazing up at him, trying to memorise every detail of his neat face, with its high cheekbones and smooth curved forehead. "But as you'll find out, all the best things are."

She'd meant only to lie there being kissed; never would she have even considered allowing anyone to undress her on the first date. And this was hardly a date – Lance hadn't even asked her out. But she'd found herself letting him pull off the cable-knit sweater her mother had knitted her and slowly unbutton the linen shirt she wore underneath to stop the wool giving her spots.

"Will you listen, Kitty," he'd said. "This is very important. You must understand one thing. I mean really understand it. Are you listening?" She'd nodded, hypnotised. "I can't offer you anything. I can't offer anyone anything. I'm incapable of falling in love. Don't

77

imagine that I'll make an exception in your case, because I won't. All I can offer you is this."

Kitty shrugged deeper into her coat as the night air bit at her neck. Jack and the stallion seemed nearly asleep, both had their eyes half-closed and their heads lowered. She should have slapped Lance's face and kicked him out of her room. The strange thing was, she'd been aware at the time that her real self, the person she'd been ever since she could remember, since she was five at least, felt like doing that, but a new self, a fairly recent self, who'd only put in an appearance in the last few years, unpredictably passionate and emotional, with feelings that wiped out rational thought like a wet sleeve dissolving equations on a blackboard, had leaned forward and sealed the contract with a kiss, and after that there was no going back.

6

Kitty could hear banging from the inner yard, and as she got closer caught a low roar and smelt singeing hair. It was a hard, frosty day with flakes of slush blowing in the wind, and a few hissed into a brazier set by the stone steps, its coals fanned by a Hoover cunningly adapted to blow instead of suck. Jack had his back to her and a long leather apron wrapped round him, the strings tied in a loop at the back; he was hammering at an anvil while the big white mare, Blossom, stood quietly by, tied to a ring in the wall. She rolled her eyes and gave a snort of distaste when she saw Kitty, but Jack was too absorbed to notice. He was making an uneven sound with his hammering, and Kitty saw he was hitting one stroke directly on the anvil and the other onto a horseshoe laid on it with a pair of giant pincers. He clicked his tongue at Blossom and backed towards her rump, giving a grunt of effort as he lifted one of her feet up and held it steady on his knees. There was a bubbling hiss as the hot shoe burned into horn and hair, but the wind wiped away the smoke and the mare didn't flinch. Instead she twisted round to see what Jack was doing, curled her lips back, and very delicately caught hold of his apron-strings with her teeth. She pulled and the loop slid undone, the apron dropping neatly over the shoe and stopping the work.

"Very clever," Jack said, putting her foot down and

straightening up, his voice teasing and affectionate. "You're such a witty little horse, aren't you?" He was reaching behind to retie the bow when he saw Kitty.

"Going to see the stallion?" he asked, his voice a little less warm.

"I thought I would."

"I've just trimmed his feet. They're so hard he don't need shoeing. He didn't appreciate them being picked up. You watch out for him: he's feeling himself today." Jack put the emphasis on the word "feeling", so his words had a mysterious quality, but Kitty took them to mean the animal was in an uncertain temper. He'd changed with the new diet. Strength was returning to him in uneven bursts, distorting his mild temperament: sometimes he'd act as if his body tingled and his skin fitted too tight, and lash out wildly; at others he'd revert to standing, head dipped, brooding on the miseries of life, a position he'd grown accustomed to in Eli's pig hut. He looked different now, after a week of careful attention: his coat had been combed free of loose hairs, the lice had gone, and his mane and tail glittered with white cream. He was still ribby, but his eyes had plumped up and gone silky from the better diet; twice a day Jack mixed a warm mash for him – a blend of bran, oats, and soaked sugar beet. There was an element of magic in the feeding of the stallion: Kitty noticed how Jack added a spoonful of powder to each feed from a golden tin so ancient the label had worn away, and Pug made great play with an odd-looking thing called a "Black Physick Ball", which he insisted on blowing down Truncheon's throat with a wooden tube. It was like a badly made marble, with a treacly, medicinal smell, and Truncheon resented it deeply, thundering with his hooves on the stable floor when he saw Pug getting out his wooden tube. Every time anyone commented on how much better the stallion looked Pug would say in a proud, serious voice, "It's the Black

Physick Ball" and crumple a paper bag meaningfully in his pocket.

Jack resumed his shoeing, and as Kitty turned away she saw Blossom lean forward again, lips peeled back, ready for another try at his apron.

Choosing the stallion's name had taken a great deal of thought.

"How about Reuben?"

"No – it's unlucky," Pug had snarled. "Williamses up the road had two Reubens and they both died come the finish."

"Captain, Major, Colonel?" Roger had continued. "Always was a Colonel on the farm in my father's day. Big bay geldings they was, with white feather I'd to brush out with sawdust every morning. I don't know, Jack, you keep talking about using the horses on the farm, but I can't see you putting in the hours I did: rising at five to groom the geldings, and falling asleep over the tack at night." He'd sat back and bitten into a fairy cake, proud of his grim youth.

"You don't have to do all that brushing," Jack had countered. "It takes the weather-proofing out their coats." He'd paused. "What do you think to Sundancer?"

"Too fancy. He'd turn nish with a name like that: keep indoors if it was raining and fuss if he got mud on his hooves."

"How about Balls' Pride?" Pug had offered. "That'd be a good strong name for a stallion."

"It has to be a name no horse round here has ever had; solid, and right for a big stallion, and short, so you can get it out quick." Jack had looked expectantly at the other two; both had had their lips pressed shut, as if scared the wrong kind of name would escape.

"Trojan," Kitty had suggested from the sink. "Like the Trojan Horse." When the company remained puzzled and silent she'd added, "It means a person who endures with courage, and he has, hasn't he?"

"It's a good name," Jack said grudgingly, "but too long for me. I can't see meself shouting it out."

"Go on, Jack," There'd been a bullying edge to Roger's voice. "Let the maid have her way. If it wasn't for her you wouldn't have the stallion."

"Education!" she'd heard Pug murmur disgustedly from the dog's room as he was leaving. "I never heard of no truncheon horse."

"Hey, Truncheon," Kitty called, and the stallion shifted uneasily in his stall. It was a silly name, but she hadn't liked to tell the men they'd misheard her. No doubt they found her voice incomprehensibly plummy. Sometimes she'd catch them winking at each other while she was speaking, which she didn't do often. She kept her remarks short, and made sure they were interesting or amusing, so it was either her accent, or the fact that she was female that was being mocked. With Pug especially, she felt she was in the presence of someone to whom women were beneath contempt. The instant she opened her mouth a look of pain would cross his face, as if she'd switched on an electric drill and was applying it to a nerve. His eyes would squeeze shut and she'd see him longing only for the agony to be over as quickly as possible. This morning, as she was icing a cake for tea – if it was covered in enough swirls of butter cream it became a gateau and could be served as a sweet – she'd heard him say, "You can't feel for a woman what you can for a man. It's different altogether." One of his eyes had been swollen and bruised, giving his words the air of coming from some repository of rough, manly wisdom. Roger had nodded his agreement, and Jack had swung backwards and forwards on his tipped-back chair.

"It's real friendship, a man's friendship," Pug had

82

continued. "Something to trust and rely on." There'd been tears in his voice. He hadn't gone into what was wrong with a woman's friendship. Maybe he would have – Kitty had put her forcing-bag down and was waiting, scarcely daring to breathe, for him to do so – if Jack hadn't suddenly banged his chair onto its two front feet, shattering the confidential mood.

"Where's this guest to, then?" Roger had asked, and it was a while before Kitty had realised he was addressing her and remembered she was still awaiting the arrival of the latest guest.

"Well, he rang the other day," she'd answered, wiping her hands on her apron. " I wrote down what he said, I've got it somewhere."

"Never mind all that; tell me what he said."

"He said he'd cricked his neck packing and felt it would be better if he lay down and rested for a fortnight."

"Cricked his neck packing, did he?" Pug had mumbled. "I'd like to see what he'd crick if we took him out hay-making."

Roger's face had reddened dangerously. "Holiday-makers!" he'd exploded. "More trouble than they're worth. Always changing their blooming minds, coming and going, grumbling and complaining. And can you get they to stay in the winter? Wouldn't think of it. They's all crowding to come in the summer, and then it isn't good enough and they moans on about the rain and cold and wants their money back."

"You stick with the Social, Roger," Pug had said soothingly.

"The Social?" Kitty had been puzzled.

"That's right. They finds old biddies what no one wants to be bothered with, but that isn't bad enough for to need the homes, like this here Mrs Riddler, and I takes they in. That kind'll stay all year round, see, and no trouble. It's good steady cash."

"You mean . . . " The thought was so horrible that Kitty had difficulty putting it into words. "You mean Miss Biffen and Mrs Ridley are here *for ever*?"

"I wouldn't say that, no, I wouldn't say that. Last lot that come in, they was only here twenty day, wasn't they, Pug?" He'd turned back to Kitty and said in a tone of withering contempt: "A little dab of rain water come in on their bed and they was gone."

Truncheon had fallen into one of his trances. He was gazing into his empty feed dish, so wrapped in thought that when a sleepy winter bluebottle flew onto his neck and walked up it he didn't even twitch. Kitty patted him gingerly on the rump, standing well out of range so if he suddenly felt like kicking her he couldn't. Jack had explained that heavy horses hated hurting humans and trampling them underfoot, and would go to some pains to avoid it, but she hadn't been convinced. She could see it would be uncomfortable for Truncheon to squash Jack, but he probably wouldn't even notice if he did it to her.

She heard Jack switch off the Hoover outside, and in the stillness that followed caught the sound of his boot heels tapping on the cobbles.

"I'm going to have a try at breaking him," he said, blocking out the light from the stable door, and added more gently: "You want to watch?"

"If you don't object."

"You've the right. He's half yours, isn't he?" There was an edge to Jack's voice, as if he'd been reminded of that fact a little too often recently. He lifted harness off the hooks on the wall behind her, and when he spoke again he sounded less hostile. "He's already halter-broke, and I ain't seen no bad habits yet. He steps in and out of the stable lively enough."

Kitty struggled up onto the wooden stall-divider and balanced there, legs swinging.

"I bought a gelding once," Jack continued, grooming Truncheon's coat with a plastic scraper, "a lovely looking horse, a big glossy brown Irish draught, dirt cheap off a travelling man, and when I got him back would he go in the stable? Would he hell. He'd stick half-way; head in and backside out, just stand there witn his ears back and a nasty look on his face. If you touched him, fire come out his mouth. Biting and carrying on, I never seen anything like it. If it wasn't for Pug and the yard brush he'd be there still – I couldn't get him out the doorway."

"What happened?"

Jack slipped a bit into Truncheon's mouth. The stallion pushed his huge tongue against the metal and nodded his head in dismay at the unfamiliar taste. Jack pushed his fingers into the animal's mouth, easing the bit more comfortably into position, and wiped the spittle off on Truncheon's shoulder. "I took him to the next auction and sold him on. It wasn't hard finding a buyer, he was a good looker. Made a profit on him, too. It wasn't more than a week later that Eli turned up with the exact same horse saying how it was just the right sort for me. I said, 'Not pissing likely!' I bet that gelding's still making the round of the dealers – that is if he hasn't gone for dog's meat."

Truncheon was resigned to the bit now. He stood patiently while Jack fastened a leather split collar round his neck, pulling the coarse grey mane free. Curved metal hames buckled on over the collar, and then Jack fastened a crupper – a long piece of leather with a loop at one end for the tail to fit through – onto the collar, threw another wide strap across the stallion's back, and threaded chains and lengths of rope through the hooks and rings attached to all these things, so Truncheon looked as if he was wearing an open-weave corset. He didn't like it when the links rattled; his eyes showed a sliver of white and he trembled.

"Why would a horse behave like that? Refuse to go in and out of a stable?"

Jack raised one eyebrow. "Any shock'd do it," he said. "A grockle might've dropped on his head when he was coming in one morning." His voice sounded amused; maybe he'd finally forgiven her for frightening Blossom. Kitty looked down from her high perch on the stall-divider and saw that he was smiling. She felt a warm blush prickle up her neck, and pretended a sudden interest in Truncheon's ears.

"Or a bee could've stung him on the throat," Jack continued, pronouncing "throat" as if it began with an f. "A shock like that and if he wasn't treated right, hesitating at the door'd become a habit and a vice."

He led the stallion into the field beyond the gate, where there was a big sawn log, its bark starred with crinkly lichen. It lay in a puddle of mud, and rolled free with a rude noise when Jack fastened a rope round it and fixed it to the draw-bar at the end of Truncheon's chains. Kitty sat on a tussock to watch and wrapped her coat round her legs.

"I wouldn't sit there if I was you," Jack said, testing the slack on the chain.

"Why ever not?"

"It's an emmet-butt, that's why," he paused to translate, "an ant hill."

Kitty leapt up with a scream and moved to a flat patch further off.

"This'll slow him down," Jack shouted into the wind. "He won't get far with this lot behind him." He clicked his tongue and Truncheon sprang forward, pulling up short as the chain tightened. The tree trunk dragged free with a crackling roar and bounced down the field after him, hurling bark and moss into the air.

Kitty felt cold and lonely when they'd gone, and a light rain began sprinkling her face. She could see them in the distance, Jack walking hurriedly behind the log, while on the other side of that rolling storm of dirt Truncheon worked himself into a frenzy of frustration, bucking and rearing, desperate to be free. She wished she could help, instead of sitting here on her own, getting wet. She couldn't really see how to participate, though. The alternatives were all equally unattractive: riding the stallion like a bucking bronco, prancing nimbly on the log as it rolled, or trotting beside Jack, getting in his way. Would he object if she walked solemnly in the rear? She was getting to her feet to find out when she noticed the rattling getting louder; they were coming back. Truncheon's stride was steady now, and there was a look of resignation, even boredom, on his face.

"Whoa!" Jack looped the reins over the gate and patted his horse delightedly. "He hardly needs breaking. First time out and he's working like a good one!" He reached to caress the horse and it twisted and bit him savagely on the shoulder. Without any hesitation whatever Jack punched it on the forehead. There was a sickening smack as the blow hit home, and the horse reared back and up, shaking with horror. "You bugger!" Jack shouted. "Don't you try that again." Truncheon dropped back onto his front hooves and dipped his head, watching Jack from the corner of one wary eye.

Kitty's hands curled into fists. "Don't you think that's cruel?" she asked, in the low, trembling voice she reserved for being furious in.

"What do you call biting me? Kind?" Jack rubbed his shoulder and winced. "Skin's broke for sure."

"I don't think he meant it. He was just cross about the log."

"He meant it all right."

The stallion shivered, and his harness jingled. Wanting to comfort him, Kitty reached up to stroke his nose, but Jack stopped her, grabbing her firmly by the wrist.

87

"No you don't," he said. "You're not patting him better. Leave him be to learn his lesson."

She wrenched her arm free. "It's wrong to hurt animals," she said fiercely. "There has to be something else you can do instead of hitting him."

"If there is I ain't come across it." Jack spoke with absolute certainty.

Kitty was puzzled by his attitude: she knew she was in the right. She remembered so vividly those warm, loving discussions at home when she had misbehaved. "I don't want to have to smack you, darling, because violence breeds violence." She held herself very straight. "Violence is always wrong," she said firmly, and turned on her heel.

"What do you want me to do, hey?" Jack called after her, his voice teasing. "Get him to say he's sorry? Ask him to write out one hundred times 'I must not be a naughty horse?'" When she didn't turn round he shouted more rudely, "And how many stallions have you broke, then?"

7

Jack didn't come into the house for a meal that day, nor in the days that followed. He was using all his free time to break the stallion, and the valley reverberated to the crackling roar of his log. From inside the house the sound had the tireless monotony of a cockchafer battling with the shutters of a darkened room, and was most intrusive before dawn, when it didn't have the generator to compete with. Kitty, who had intended to ignore Jack until he promised to treat the stallion more kindly, found herself waking early and searching from her window for a flicker of movement as he trundled up and down in the field beside the stable.

After a week he began to work the two horses together. He coupled them up side by side to a mat of twisted metal called a chain harrow, and set them to pulling it across the grass. The top side of the stable field was overhung with trees, and Kitty crept out there one evening and hid in the undergrowth to watch. It wasn't too bad among the leaf mould and bracken stalks, provided she forgot about insects crawling up her trouser legs. She patted a pile of leaves and earth into a low mound and folded her arms on it, lying flat on her stomach and resting her pointed chin on one wrist. Above her she could hear pigeons rustling in the leafless trees as they settled for the night.

The horses looked even bigger when you were lying

flat on the ground, and at first she was only conscious of how powerful their legs were as they passed and repassed in front of her. Then she began to notice their relationship. Truncheon was the wider, stronger-looking horse; beside him Blossom looked narrow and bony apart from her fat stomach, yet she was definitely in command. She walked a few steps ahead of him, pulling him along with the harness that linked their mouths together. He didn't like the feeling of being in the harrow, and he was resentful, but he had to keep walking, Blossom never let up for a moment.

Jack strode along behind, the long reins in his hands, calling out instructions: "Easy, Blossom, easy", "Get on there, boy", and "Off back around, off back around", as they turned at each end of the field. This was a very graceful movement when Blossom did it. She walked in a wide circle, forwards and sideways at the same time, crossing her legs at knees and hocks, engaging in the kind of stately dance Kitty had seen circus horses perform, her white mane and tail floating in the wind. Truncheon dragged along behind her, and when she paused after a turn, waiting for the call, "Walk on, Blossom, walk on, boy", before leaning into her collar, he suddenly rebelled. He'd had enough of being pulled round the field by a bossy old mare. He wasn't taking another step. He twisted to one side and dipped his head, his body planted firmly on the ground, every sinew under his scruffy coat tense with rebellion. His ears were pricked, and Kitty fancied she saw his eyes shine with wicked joy.

Jack clicked his tongue and slapped the end of the reins against the stallion's buttocks, but it didn't have any effect. "Get on, you bugger!" he shouted, and threw a small clod of earth that bounced off Truncheon's neck. When that didn't work either, he weighed the reins in his hand, considering whether to go round and pull the stallion from in front. Blossom sensed his uncertainty and twisted her head round to give him a swift look. Then she leaned across and bit her partner on the neck.

He squealed and flung back his head, and launched himself into a miniature tantrum of bucking and kicking, restrained from moving very far by the harness that linked him to Blossom. She stood quite still, her head down and her eyes closed, as if she found his behaviour inexpressibly wearisome. When he'd finished, and stood huffing in the harness, turning his head with little jolts from side to side to see what was going to happen next, Jack clicked his tongue.

"Get on, boy."

Blossom opened her eyes and looked at the stallion, and since he didn't show any sign of moving she wrinkled her lips and stretched out for another bite. It was enough; he gave in at once and jogged forward, and they were off again, dragging the harrow across the field. And this time, unless Kitty was mistaken, he was keeping up with the mare, his step hasty as he tried to avoid the indignity of being pulled.

Kitty thought it clever and economical of Jack to get Blossom to do his breaking for him. When he unharnessed the two carthorses and set them free she waited to see if Truncheon bore the mare any malice for the bite, but instead he was extra deferential. He lingered shyly by the gate until she'd finished drinking at the trough, and didn't find the courage to slake his own thirst until she'd gone to graze in her favourite corner. Jack watched them, too, a lonely figure, leaning on the gate and slapping the empty bridles against the palm of his hand. Truncheon nuzzled him with a dripping mouth before drifting, with adolescent shyness, as close to Blossom's sway-backed white body as he dared.

Kitty felt cold, but she stayed where she was until smoke began flowing from the chimney of Jack's hut. The moon was up, and as she struggled out of the dead bracken she saw the gander on tiptoe, tasting the froth the horses had left behind on the water trough. She made a wide circle to avoid him, and caught a movement by the stone steps in the inner yard. It was the goose creeping out of a hole in the brickwork. She gave a cackle and squeezed under the gate to join her husband.

There was an ancient dog kennel hollowed out of the base of the step, with a fan of bricks above its entrance. Kitty had never noticed it before. That must be where the geese slept. She knew they weren't shut in at night, there was no need; Roger had re-enacted for her, with sound effects, the legendary occasion when a fox had tried to scrag the gander. The kennel was stuffed with farm rubbish – old sacks, broken bricks, corrugated iron – and in the middle was a heap of white feathers. It might have been an effect of the moonlight, but Kitty thought some of the feathers looked too dark and wide to come from a goose. She reached in and pulled one out. It wasn't a feather. It was a torn strip of airmail paper, covered in familiar black copperplate. She felt around for some more, then carried them over to the big yard, where the storm light on the wall was bright enough to read by.

. . . better than I could get rearing young stock. I saw Philip last week, up across the fields talking to Rog. Rog was sat stock still on the tractor seat and Philip leaning on the step. I would know him anywhere, the way he holds himself. I asked Rog what it was about and he said Philip was coming back to be married and wanted him for best man. I said You never will, but he said My answer was yes.

Shaking with excitement, Kitty looked at the next piece, this time a complete letter.

Dear Hilda,

I have been lonely the last few months. Since old Mrs S. passed on I have missed the company. I am writing this in the kitchen. Rog has gone on to bed, but I am too tired to sleep. I lifted sixty sacks of spuds on my own today. They were terribly cut about, I have never seen them so bad.

Deborah May's sentences were stiff and abrupt, but somehow the scenes they described became vivid to Kitty. She forgot she was standing in a farmyard, forgot the washing-up she still had to do before the generator was switched off, and became totally absorbed in the other woman's life, reading the neat, regular handwriting and supplying the thoughts she sensed between the lines.

The turned earth stretched away before her, Rog's tractor ticking over beside the gate. He unhitched the spinner and set it down by the hedge, leaving the engine running. "Don't do that, it's dangerous," Deborah called, but her words were blown away. She stooped and grubbed out more potatoes with her rubber gloves. Best for her to do this; you couldn't trust him to get it right. He'd leave too many in to seed next spring. She frowned. The potatoes were never this cut about when her dad span them. Rog couldn't do anything decent, he was useless. She felt like screaming at him at times, but there wasn't any point. The things you said when you felt like that could never be forgotten. She still remembered the day he'd shouted, "I should never have taken you on. Secondhand goods!" She hated everything about him: his long yellow toe nails, the soft way he looked when his clothes were off, his body bent round to protect his precious shrivelled staff that had never been any good either. Sometimes in the night he'd reach out a hand to touch her and she'd go stiff, willing him to stop. How could he even think of it, when he was the way he was in the day? Never talking to her or looking at her, treating her as a servant – a dog more like – with no feelings at all to respect.

She stooped lower, so a blunt pain nagged at the base of her spine. It wasn't bad, she could bear it. She was used to going on when her body was playing up. Men might be stronger, but women had the endurance. That was five bags, not bad for a row, but then this side of the field always grew better, it was the bad drainage that did it, the potatoes were grateful for the extra water.

It was good to be in the fresh air, she hated the indoors. Sad voices called from above and Haskins's geese flapped over. They did that every evening, going back to his lake. Made it himself, he had, and earned a fair bit from the fishing. Rog ought to do the same, and use up the bad land, but he never would get round to it. He liked to take his time. Look how long their engagement had been: nine years, ever since she turned sixteen. He was the choice her father wanted: good bit of land to him, known his family for five generations, and who else was there? Seemed like everyone in the village paired up in their cradles. Of course, he'd never looked much beside Philip, but then nobody did. She'd not minded Rog back at the beginning, he was a short, sturdy lad then, terrible how he'd aged. It seemed to her that he'd always been nasty, only she hadn't seen it at first. Marriage for her was like a curtain being slowly jerked aside, revealing the other in all their weakness and dishonour. The first time the curtain was moved was when she had just come out of the hospital with Jack, and Rog had a heifer down and calving. She was too weak to help, it'd been a hard labour and the doctor had made her promise not to stir from her bed for a week. Rog couldn't get the calf out of the heifer, and he was too mean to send for the veterinary. He lost his head, tied the calf's feet to the tractor, and started the engine. Of course he killed the both of them, cow and calf. How he could have done that, when he'd seen her in labour, and right outside her window, too; well, that showed what kind of man he was.

94

There were only two more pieces of letter.

. . . sad not even to get a card from you. Whatever
I have done I think it cruel of you not to write.
When the post comes I always think there will be a
letter from you but Rog holds it in his hand and
says, "Not today girl," as if he is pleased to hurt my
feelings.

We had a good Christmas. Philip and his new
wife spent the day. I had to laugh because they had
a big toy tractor for Jack, that he could ride on, and
Rog only bought him a rubber ball!

Philip's wife is the kind to turn heads anywhere . . .

*Deborah didn't want to like her. She wanted to warm herself at
the thought that Philip had made a bad choice, but it didn't
turn out like that. His wife was as pretty as a doll, and yet she
put no value on herself. When she told how she'd met Philip
she didn't say she'd been the one courted, no, she'd had a
terrible fight to snatch him from a whole pack of jealous
women. She loved him fiercely and never tired of talking about
him. Deborah could ask her any question and have it answered
with a lively acting out of what he'd said and done. It was
these talks that made them friends: they soothed a need they
both had, to be close to someone, a need Philip refused to
satisfy.*

. . . the supper and the men were rowdy with
drink. I was early to bed with Jack and I could hear
them singing in the parlour . . .

*The men were making too much noise for her to sleep. She
dressed again and went down to sit with them. Rog was lolling
from side to side, telling the story he always told when he'd
had a glass too many, all about his brother being kicked to
death by the Shire they had then, and how none of the family*

could ever abide a horse after. Philip stopped singing, and he stared into the fire for a long while. She was glad he was drunk because then he wouldn't mind her looking at him. If she did it in the day he stared her down, angry, meaning, "You leave me alone." Now he started saying, his voice louder than he wanted it to be, "I'm sorry, I'm so sorry" over and over again. He wasn't saying it to her, the woman he'd betrayed and left, he was saying it to Rog. When his hand touched Rog's and they both set to crying she went back upstairs and put the pillow against her ears.

Kitty dreamt about the geese all that night, and the next morning woke to hear them shrieking outside her window, their voices more muffled than usual. She sat up and opened the curtains. The air was white with a sea mist, and drops of moisture trembled on the ivy leaves under her sill. It must be late; she could hear Roger riddling the stove in the kitchen below, and the thud as he threw quartered logs into the firebox. He always lit it for her after he'd finished the milking, so the hob was hot for breakfast, and all through the day he'd come in and top it up, and open and close the dampers. He never made her feel he was reproaching her for being unable to cope; instead he'd scowl into the firebox, as if checking that it had been behaving itself decently in his absence. It was like the way he always ate her meals with stoic dedication, however disgusting they might be. She found it hard to reconcile such kindness and tact with the monster who'd deliberately not posted Deborah May's letters.

She had meant to creep up on the goose kennel and snatch a few more of those letters under cover of the mist, but when she got outside she was distracted by hearing a lamb cry, high up in the cup of the hills. It sounded terrified and desperate, and she climbed over the fence beside the yard and began walking in the direction it had come from. The older lambs were out here now with their mothers, and as she stumbled along she hit clear patches in the mist and saw them dozing under the hedges. She smiled as she skirted two plump lambs curled up asleep on their mother's back.

Half-way up the field she passed a gate that had been ripped out of its opening, crushed, and thrown to one side, but its significance escaped her until she reached the top, and stopped to catch her breath. She was very close to the trees here, they loomed up like jagged mountains in the mist, and she realised it was silly to have worried about the lamb; there was a ewe close at hand, her deep voice melting with love and reassurance. Then the mist parted into threads and Kitty saw a pale shape ahead of her. She blinked. It was Truncheon. He was pointing into the corner of the field, his head dipped low, and as she watched he raised it abruptly, his mane a ripple of smoke, and she heard a soft thud. She leaned forward to see what he was doing. The old sheep she'd lambed over a month ago with Jack's help, Cankerlug, was backed up against the fence. She looked frail compared to the huge stallion, but that didn't stop her staring fiercely at him, her golden eyes dark against the mist, and stamping one neat brown-trimmed foot so hard the ground trembled. When he didn't retreat she lowered her head, ready to butt, and Truncheon lifted one hoof delicately at the knee and kicked her on the crown.

For a moment Kitty was frozen, unable to make immediate sense of what she'd seen. The stallion's movements were so graceful, and she'd always thought of cruelty as freakish and clumsy, an unnatural kind of behaviour. Then she rushed at him, flapping her hands, her instinctive fear forgotten.

"You bad, bad horse!" she shouted. "Stop it at once!" He wheeled round and trotted lightly off, pausing to graze just a few yards away. "Whoosh!" she shouted, and ran at him again, until he'd melted into the mist.

97

Cankerlug shook her head, as if she thought the pain was crouching on top and could be flicked off, then bent and licked at the lamb beside her. It struggled fatly, but couldn't get up. One leg was broken.

Kitty hardly noticed her feet hitting the ground as she ran back down the field. She didn't know how to cope with the outrage she felt at what the stallion had done, her body was swollen with it; her head felt tight and hot. She averted her head as she passed the smashed gateway. Truncheon was poised there like a ghost, and she couldn't bear to look at him.

She found Jack beside his hut, talking to Blossom while he oiled the axle of his cart. The mare's head was only just visible in the whiteness, leaning over the hedge, a twig dangling from her lips like a cigarette, and Jack was saying softly:

"This isn't for you, you old baggage. You're too far on now for shafts. And when are you going to come up with the goods, hey? I'm waiting."

They both looked up, annoyed, when Kitty coughed, and she was made to feel she'd interrupted an intimate moment.

"Cankerlug's lamb's got a broken leg," she burst out. "And I think . . . " It was almost too terrible to put into words, and she faltered, "I think Truncheon might have done it."

"I been giving him too much corn, that's what it is," Jack answered. "I thought he was getting too full of his self."

"Then you think he did do it?"

"It wouldn't surprise me. I've caught him huffing up the gander's tail-feathers before now, spoiling for a fight, and he's been eyeing up those lambs. How'd he get in? Rubbed down the gate with his backside?"

Kitty was incensed by Jack's calmness, the way he was rolling the cart back and forth, checking the free-running of the wheels while he spoke, as if the matter didn't deserve his full attention. How could he be like that, when a dreadful crime had just been committed on his farm?

"Why aren't you angry with him?" she cried. "Is it because he only injured a lamb? You were angry enough when it was you that got hurt."

"I've had it up to here with you telling me what to do with my stallion." Jack spoke with menace, and he held the edge of his hand to his throat as he said "here". "First it was 'Oh no, you mustn't be cruel'; now it's 'Why don't you lay into him with a big stick?'" His voice rose to a fruity falsetto when he imitated Kitty.

She looked at the ground, and dug her fingernails into her palms, refusing to be goaded. She wanted to know the answers too badly to back away. "You're not being fair," she said. "I'm not saying you've got to hit him. I just don't think he should be allowed to get away with it."

"We been here before. The only way to stop him is to give him a clout when he does it."

Kitty thought of the fat little lamb struggling and twisting on its back in the mist, and she saw Blossom's big teeth, with their wide, bubble-gum-pink gums, bared ready to bite. "Well – maybe. Maybe you've got a point," she said slowly. "I suppose in some circumstances that's not entirely indefensible." She didn't like giving way, but she wasn't sure any more whether the same rules of behaviour applied to horses as to people, and it didn't seem right to stick rigidly to a principle she had reservations about. Maybe it was a result of reading Deborah May's letters, but she couldn't help feeling resentful that she should always have to give way to men. Why couldn't they be the ones to change their opinions occasionally? Jack was watching her, his eyes narrowed, and his coldness made her uncomfortable. "Why don't you go and do something about Truncheon, then?" she said, her voice tearful.

"It's too late. He's gone and got away with it. If I'd've been there when he did it I'd've sorted him out good and proper, but there's no point now, he wouldn't know what I was carrying on about."

"What I don't understand is why he did it in the first place. He must be truly evil, mustn't he, to enjoy hurting another animal? And he did look as if he was enjoying it. That was what was so horrible."

"He's young. Playful. And he's a stallion. He'll do a lot worse before he's through." Jack wiped his oily hands on his shirt before resting them on the side of the cart, then rocked a little from side to side, as he sorted out in his mind what he wanted to say. After a pause he began quietly: "No one's perfect. You can't expect a horse that size to be an angel. Everyone does, though. 'Gentle giants', that's what they call heavies. It makes me want to urge.

"I took Blossom to a show back along, thought she might bring in a bit of prize money. The way the grockles at that show carried on! Putting their babies' hands in her mouth, letting little kids crawl about under her legs? You never seen anything like it. And they would have gone screaming mad if she'd've trod on one of them, not that it would have been her fault. The way they saw her had shit all to do with what she was. They thought she was . . . made out of plastic. A chocolate box come to life." Jack swallowed.

"I'll tell you – I was out in the ring, waiting for the judge. It was hot, and I was parched. I daren't leave the mare, not with all those plonkers about, and I had to have a drink. She was nursing – I'd left her foal at home, good job too, as it turned out – and I could see her bag getting tight. So I thought: why not do the both of us a good turn? You never *seen* the carrying on there was when I bent down and helped meself to a drink of milk. Ordered us off the showground and all. Disgrace to the county – you can imagine. It's like those plonkers live in a different world."

"I don't want to live in a different world." Kitty had been giggling at the story, but she was serious now.

"The stallion's a good sort, but he's got bad in him too. That's not so unusual."

There was a silence as they smiled at each other across the cart. Kitty could tell Jack was completely unaware of how beautiful he was. All the handsome men she'd seen before had unconsciously posed when they were being watched, and their faces had looked well-fingered from hours of examination in a mirror. Jack's appearance was entirely separate from his character, like a polished shield held up in front, that dazzled others but left him unaffected. Blossom snorted. "Pooh!" she said in disgust.

"I'm trying the stallion in a cart tomorrow," Jack said. "You want to come along?"

"Is it safe?"

"Soon find out if it isn't."

8

"Are you sure it isn't too difficult for him?" Kitty asked, as she balanced on the frozen waves of mud by the yard gate.

"He'll do it," Jack murmured, engrossed in persuading the stallion to walk backwards between the tipped-down shafts of the cart.

Now Truncheon had rounded out a little he looked childish and stocky. He was more solemn this morning than she'd ever seen him, his dark eyes thoughtful as he tried to understand what Jack wanted him to do. His upper eyelashes were thick and black, those on the bottom not growing on a lid but curving singly out of the skin a little below the eye, like whiskers.

Jack held him gently by his muzzle, that was as white against the rest of the strawberry-roan coat as if it had been dipped in milk, and pushed him back into the narrow space between the shafts. Over and over again the stallion managed only a couple of steps before treading on a shaft with a bang that rattled the metal fittings, but each time Jack soothed him, drew him forward and tried again. He never lost his patience, and the stallion didn't get restless either. Every time he stumbled he'd raise his head and a look of understanding would cross his face, as if each blunder helped him to imagine the space behind him with greater accuracy.

Kitty wandered over to the back door, fiddling with

her apron, and worried about whether the house looked clean enough. Roger had gone to market, and the new guest, Geoff Jiggins, was expected at any moment. She wasn't looking forward to showing him his room: he'd probably reel back in outrage. The worst feature was the small felt cushion she'd had to position in the middle of the bedspread to hide the hole.

"Good boy. Clever boy, aren't you, hey?" She looked up. Truncheon was standing in position at last, a mist of sweat rising from his legs and stomach. Jack lifted the shafts to chest level, and keeping them steady, dodged left to throw a chain over the wooden pad on the stallion's back, then right to catch it and hook it onto a shaft-fitting. While he fastened links and buckles Kitty scrambled into the cart.

Jack laughed. "There's no hurry," he said. "He's not going anywhere fast."

He took Truncheon by the bridle and led him forward. The stallion went willingly, glad to have an easy task for a change, but stopped, puzzled, after only a couple of steps. His movement had turned the wheels of the cart and set the shafts moving on either side of his body. The harness holding him within those shafts enclosed him on all sides, like a leather net, and when the cart moved it rubbed tight. Kitty saw him shrink from its touch, and he lowered his head, trembling with fear and dismay. He didn't want to move again.

"It's all right, boy," Jack said gently, "I'm here, and I won't let anything hurt you." He pulled on the bridle and the horse took little teetering steps beside him, stopping anxiously whenever the cart began rolling.

"Would it be easier for him if I got off?" Kitty asked. Jack shook his head. He couldn't reply because he was too busy talking to the horse. They were at the yard gate now, and Jack opened it and led Truncheon through into the meadow. Most of the sheep were still asleep, but a few had moved. Kitty noticed clear ovals in the frosty grass where they'd been, like the dry patches you see in city streets when parked cars have moved on after a downpour. One or two stood up and stretched as the stallion walked past, but he took no notice of them, lost in his private misery.

The cart rattled over a bump in the grass, and the brass fittings on the harness jingled, and Truncheon began to walk faster, trying to escape from the sound. As his pace became brisker the cart bounced more vigorously, the wheels juddered, and the brass sang out. It was like a noisy demon clinging to his sides, and he couldn't bear it any longer, he had to get away. He began to trot, eyes wide and head raised, and Jack caught him and forced him to a standstill.

"Easy! You'll only make it worse on yourself. Quieten down, hey?" Jack stood beside Truncheon and waited until his breathing was calmer, and the tension had gone from his body, then walked him up towards the trees so slowly that the cart's movements were barely perceptible. They passed Cankerlug on the way: her lamb was wearing a splint covered in a plastic fertiliser bag, and hopped hastily to one side.

Half-way up, Jack, judging the horse to be a little more at ease, swung up next to Kitty in the cart. Truncheon walked carefully ahead, his pose as dejected as if he was dragging a weight of guilt behind him, his ears swivelled back to hear what Jack was saying, and if the flow of soothing words stopped he'd turn his head, in the most touching way possible, to check that Jack was still there.

Truncheon didn't like turning to right or to left, and Kitty could see why. He was enclosed in a moving box, and to turn had to press against what seemed to him a solid obstruction. It was a dreadful, claustrophobic situation to put him in, and watching him cringe from the touch of the shafts, but nevertheless keep walking in order to please Jack, she felt both admiration and pity.

Something green was moving on the edge of her vision: it was a shiny car weaving round the cracks in the drive.

"I have to go now," she said to Jack.

He looked at her, dazed; he'd been concentrating so hard on the stallion that he'd forgotten she was there.

Mr Jiggins had disappeared indoors when she reached the house. The taxi was sliding back up the hill, and she could see pointed footprints leading away from a puddle in the yard. They wandered into the kitchen, round the dining room table, across the lounge – where they made a slight detour to stand beside Miss Biffen's knitting bag – and out into the hall. Mr Jiggins appeared to have very elaborate shoes: the soles were covered in wiggles and stars. She found him at the top of the stairs, examining the Snell calendar so closely that his nose touched the paper.

He was a small man, dressed in an old-fashioned grey suit, with a smudge of moustache on his upper lip. It was his neatness that impressed her most: she'd forgotten that men could be so dapper. The paisley handkerchief puffing out of his pocket exactly matched his socks and tie.

"Mrs Snell!" he cried. "How wonderful to be here at last!" She tried to explain that she wasn't Mrs Snell, but she wasn't sure he heard; he was too involved in describing the window box outside his high-rise flat, and a nut-feeder he'd devised to test the intellectual capacity of a blue tit to its absolute limit.

"Would you like to see your room first, or shall I make you a cup of coffee?" she offered, when he paused for breath.

"I've seen my room," he replied. There was an awkward pause before he admitted that he would like some coffee and followed her into the kitchen. He stood beside her while she made it, bending from the waist

105

and poking his head forward to get a closer view. If she'd seen his face in a photograph she'd have thought it quite ordinary, but close to its colouring was odd. Most of his skin was white and close-textured, with a bloom of moisture on it, like a fresh mushroom, but where it sank into the nostrils it went a brilliant, inflamed purple.

He took a sip of his coffee and grinned at her, and she noticed his gums were seeping blood. "How old would you say I was?" he asked suddenly.

It was hard to tell. He wasn't young, but he didn't exactly look old, either. His face didn't seem used enough. He looked instead as if he'd been stored in a broom cupboard since early adolescence; he even smelt like it, too, of furniture polish, mildew, and Hoover dust. Kitty couldn't help noticing because he'd sat uncomfortably close.

"Forty-three," he said. "And I still have a full head of hair. Feel it. Go on, have a feel." He inclined his head towards her, and she put out a reluctant hand and touched his hair. It was short, but stiff and dense, like a miniature box hedge, and though it was brown it had a curious green glint in its depths. "Do you want to know my secret?" he inquired. She wasn't entirely sure she did, but it would be impolite to say no.

"I never wash it. Never."

"What do you do, then?" Despite herself, Kitty was interested.

"I take my fingers like this." Mr Jiggins pinched together the thumb and forefinger on each hand. "And I run them over my hair, grooming each strand in turn." He plucked rapidly at his head in demonstration, and for perhaps fifteen seconds there was only a dry rustle as he worked away, and a faint odour of Parmesan cheese. When he'd finished and wiped his fingers thoroughly on his handkerchief he explained to Kitty how bad washing was for the hair follicles, how it

106

stripped them of essential oils. He cited many examples of people he knew with healthy, unwashed follicles, and Kitty was particularly impressed by his description of his mother. She'd apparently had waist-length chestnut hair into her seventies, and brushed it a thousand times a day. Kitty found herself wondering whether this philosophy extended to the care of the skin, too. Maybe Mr Jiggins buffed himself to a shine each morning with a chamois leather instead of bathing. If he did it would make the bathroom arrangements a lot simpler.

He began talking about how wonderful his mother was, how lonely he'd been since she'd died, and Kitty found it a dismal monologue. She'd quite enjoyed his company when he was being peculiar, but now he was being just like anybody else, and putting on a sepulchral, self-pitying tone, she itched to escape.

"No, I've never married, never found anyone who'd have me! Well, I did have a friend once but mother didn't like her. Said she didn't look clean enough." He looked away here, as if struggling to find the courage to continue. "I suppose I should have put my foot down. I wouldn't be so lonely now if I had." When he lifted his head he moved it closer to Kitty and she could see a dark spot clinging to the white of his left eye. It wasn't flat, it seemed three-dimensional, as if he'd rolled a small dead spider into a ball and stuck it there. "That's why I decided to come on a farm holiday, because I was so desperately lonely. I felt sure that in a family home people wouldn't be able to avoid me and make me feel unwelcome."

The same thought had just that moment occurred to Kitty, too. She pushed back her chair. "Would you excuse me?" she asked. "I need to go upstairs for a moment."

"Of course." Mr Jiggins blushed as deeply as if he'd dipped his head in strawberry juice, and feeling a little ashamed of her behaviour, Kitty crept up to the bathroom and locked herself in. As she did so she wondered whether she'd stumbled on the reason Mrs Ridley spent so much time in there: it was the only place she could escape from Miss Biffen.

The mottled glass window was hazy with frost; she threw it open and leaned out. She could see Jack and Truncheon going along the edge of the field, neither one of them more than an inch high. She wished she could be out there with them, the house felt like a prison to her now. She could see, even from this distance, that Truncheon was moving more easily and confidently: his crest curved proudly and his feet were stepping high.

Someone was walking up the hill towards the horse and cart in a strange, jerky manner, prancing up and down with each step and bending forward, so that it looked as if invisible strings were pulling him up by the seat of the trousers. It was Geoff Jiggins. He wandered in front of the stallion and Kitty saw him gesture with his arms, waving them wildly round his head.

Jack pulled Truncheon to a halt and shook his fist, and Geoff shrugged and reached up to touch the horse on the nose. There was a high whinny, and then Truncheon reared, the cart tipped right back, and Kitty saw Jack fall off the side. She almost overbalanced on the sill in her desperation to see what was happening. The stallion dropped back onto his front hooves, Mr Jiggins ran, spider-like, towards the trees, and there was a moment when the situation hung in the balance. Truncheon seemed to freeze, waiting for a warning tug on his bridle, and when it didn't come he flattened his ears, stretched out his neck, and bolted. Kitty saw him gallop down towards the yard gate, the cart bouncing high in the air behind him and a bundle rolling at the end of his reins.

She snatched open the bathroom door and tumbled

down the stairs, blood thumping in her ears. All was silent except for the beating of her heart, and the house and farmyard narrowed to a long cylinder through which she was running far too slowly. The first thing she saw when she reached the gate was Truncheon, his coat dark with moisture, the hairs glued together in thick flakes. His breathing was even more laboured than hers, and he reeked of his unique perfume: bitter and musky, just on the borderline between pleasant and unpleasant, like the hard base note of human sweat. The cart was battered, but still attached to his sides, and the reins were stretched tight. She followed them back to where Jack lay face-down in the grass, one hand outstretched and still clutching the end of a rein, blood welling up from it and puddling on the frozen ground. She knelt down and rolled him over. His face was scratched and muddy, the eyes closed, and she patted at it foolishly with her hands.

"Jack! Please be all right. Please."

She felt his free arm press on her back, pushing her towards him, and without warning he kissed her. His lips were very soft and warm, and the huge arm round her made her feel totally enveloped. She'd always felt separate from Lance, even at their closest moments, but here, just with a kiss, she felt she'd almost become part of Jack. His lips opened and he kissed her more deeply, his mouth so much more cushiony than she was used to, and tasting unfamiliarly salt. She lost herself in the pleasure of it, and after a long time he released her.

"Hey," he smiled, eyes half-closed. "I got to see to the horse, I can't lie here all day." He rolled back on his stomach and inched himself towards his hand; he didn't seem able to release the rein. Kitty lay curled up on the grass, watching him as he unfolded his fist and freed a strong trickle of blood. He sucked in a breath. "It would happen to me pissing right hand."

"What?"

"I cut these reins from scrap leather and went and left a snap-crook on the end. It's stuck in me finger." He prodded at it with his other hand and winced.

"Can I help?"

"No – it's nothing. I done it now." The rein fell to the ground and Truncheon shifted by the gate. Jack felt in his back pocket and pulled out a filthy handkerchief, glued together with snot.

Kitty sat up, appalled. "You can't use that!" She wished she had a filmy petticoat on that she could tear into strips to staunch the wound, but since she'd been at Balls Farm clothes had ceased to be anything but a means of keeping warm. She had on a thermal vest and an Aran sweater Lance had particularly disliked: hard and knobbly, like a suit of armour. Neither could be reduced to strips without a buzz saw, and she could hardly use her jeans or pants.

"You're losing a lot of blood," she said severely, as her white socks matted crimson round his hand. "You really must see a doctor." She held the improvised bandage on with her fingers, liking the feel of Jack's skin, but he was impatient to get the stallion safely back in the stable.

"I don't know how I'm to get to a doctor," he said, catching Truncheon's bridle with his good hand.

"Isn't there a car somewhere?"

"It's not a car, it's a Land Rover, and the old man's taken it to market, hasn't he?" He led the tired stallion inside its stall and flicked the sweat off its coat with a scraper. "We'll sort you out," he said gently. "Soon have you warm and dry. That daft grockle got you wound up good and proper, didn't he?"

"What did he do?"

"Spooked him. He didn't like the arms going round, but it was more than that. There's some plonkers horses can't stick at any price. They don't have to do nothing, just the smell of them'll set a horse off. It's ace, the way

110

that sort all come here for their pissing bed and breakfast."

"Would Pug take you to the doctor? Can I ring him for you?"

"He's at market too. You could ring his missus. Sherry Pugh she's called. She's in the book." Just as Kitty turned to go he added: "It's not as bad as it could be. He's had a fright, but I was behind him all the way. If I'd've let go I'd've blown it, but now he knows no matter how hard he tries he can't never get away from me.

"It was just chance about the snap-crook, but if you use your head you can get good to come out of even a bad accident. A friend of mine had a horse bolt into a brick wall, and just before it hit head-on, he shouted 'Whoa'. Horse knocked his self out of course, but when he come round you just had to *whisper* 'Whoa' and he'd stop on a sixpence."

9

In a corner, near the shadowed bar, was a low table laid with two settings for tea, the cups inverted on their saucers, and Kitty could see why Miss Biffen and Mrs Ridley enjoyed sitting at it in the afternoons. The room was hot, cosy, and aggressively clean. Firelight winked off thousands of horse brasses pegged to the beams and polished to a white glitter, and the red wallpaper was half-hidden behind gold-framed photographs, all of horses pulling implements while men in smocks posed fiercely beside them. Glass chinked behind the bar and Sherry Pugh came out with a tall glass of an opaque yellow liquid that looked like custard.

"Here, have a snort," she said, and set it on a cardboard coaster in front of Kitty. "The men'll be back any time now. You'll stay to lunch, won't you? Rog can take you back after."

Jack was walking round the room, examining the photographs, his arm in a sling. He'd needed five stitches, and the doctor had told him his finger would never have any sensation in it again.

"Just my luck," Jack had said in the car on the way back. "It was my courting finger and all." Kitty couldn't see the joke, but Sherry had giggled for a long time, her body trembling like a jelly in the driver's seat. She was an enormous woman, inflating a long dress of dazzlingly fluffy pink wool, and her boots fascinated Kitty: they

112

were the most erotic she'd ever seen: palest pink trimmed with red feathers, and impossibly small and high-heeled. She felt shabby and drab by comparison, and glanced anxiously at Jack to see if he agreed, but he was still looking at the photographs, twitching his lips as he read the captions. He'd been oddly distant since that kiss; she couldn't puzzle it out. He didn't exactly behave as if nothing had happened – his attitude towards her had shifted, becoming subtly proprietorial – but he didn't seem to want to hold her hand or discuss his feelings. As for her, she was confused. Before the kiss she'd been fascinated by him, but not sure she liked him; now, while she sipped the sickly drink Sherry had given her, she couldn't help watching him out of the edge of her eye, and marvelling at the perfection of his big, muscular body and the black hair curling over his collar. Sherry smiled and Kitty blushed; she had the disconcerting feeling the other woman had guessed her thoughts. She instinctively liked Sherry, though she couldn't have said why: her face wasn't nearly as attractive as her clothes – it was hard and weathered, with small, piggy eyes.

"We hardly see Jack nowadays," Sherry said, raising her voice to call out: "Isn't that right, Jack? We hardly see you?"

"I'm working so hard, see," he murmured, his back still turned.

A dimple hollowed itself out on one of Sherry's cheeks. "He's a bit of a ladies' man, Jack is. He's like a tomcat, has to go far afield to find what he wants."

"What are you saying?" Jack's voice was mock-angry. "I can see I'll have to come back here to stop you sounding off." He sat on the settle next to Kitty, resting his good arm along the back, and quite incidentally, behind her. "How's trade?" he asked Sherry, and they began a lengthy banter in which neither was particularly clever, but both relished each other's clumsy wit. Kitty

113

was aware only of the tips of Jack's fingers brushing her shoulder as he leaned forward to parry another teasing riposte. She felt annoyed with herself. She wasn't supposed to feel like that about anyone but Lance. What kind of person was she, to start forgetting an important love affair so soon? She got up and went over to the fire with her drink, looking for somewhere to hide it. She debated pouring it into a wooden ledge on the darts board, but didn't dare; the trouble with being as houseproud as Sherry was that made it impossible for people to be tactful.

As she was eyeing a bowl of pot-pourri a horn tootled outside and Sherry said: "That'll be Puggie; I'll see to the veg," and squeezed herself through the bar door. Jack held out his hand without looking round.

"Here, give it me," he said. "She throws a wobbly if you don't finish what she gives you." Kitty passed him the glass and he downed it in one. "That's cack, that is," he commented, wiping off a yellow moustache. "Real horrible cack."

Roger looked unfamiliarly prosperous in a dark brown suit and dun shirt. He had a tweed overcoat on top, the shoulders dusted with frost, and his hair had been smoothed carefully to one side; the comb marks were still visible. As he stood by the fire Kitty smelt beer on him, and an aftershave so old its perfume had fallen into sour sections and a bitter witch hazel prevailed.

"Stock's all well?" he questioned, thick eyebrows raised, and Jack was given no sympathy for his injury, just told he was a fool for trying to break a horse on his own. Kitty noticed that none of the men ever referred to the stallion as 'Truncheon'; her unsuitable suggestion had ensured that like the God of the Old Testament, his name was lodged respectfully in the memory but never mentioned.

"Pug'd have given you a hand, all you had to do was ask." Roger settled himself at a low table and draped a

114

serviette over his knee just as Pug appeared from the kitchen with a grey plastic serving-dish of brussels sprouts. Pug's black eye had faded to palest tan, and he looked sour and shrunken, well under half the size he appeared in the Snell kitchen. "She says to tell you there's a parsley sauce on its way," he muttered, flapping back through the swing door to the kitchen.

"There's room here, young lady," Roger patted the chair next to him, and Kitty slid reluctantly onto it, suppressing the urge to look across at Jack. "If I'd have thought, I'd have asked you if you wanted a ride out to market. It'd do you good to taste a bit of fresh air. You don't want to keep indoors all day." Kitty had the uneasy feeling Roger was about to pinch her cheek or buttock in a jovial, avuncular manner, but he didn't, because Jack said provocatively:

"She's always working for you, isn't she, so when's she going to find time to go out?" He shook a lock of black hair out of his eyes and winked at Pug as he scuttled in with a dish of roast potatoes. The table was rapidly filling up with vegetable garnishes.

"There's nothing to stop her going out mornings or afternoons. Women's work's not what you'd call hard, is it?"

"What isn't hard?" Sherry loomed massively over the table, platters of gammon fanned in her fingers, and the argument died.

The meal tasted delicious, far better than anything Kitty had prepared during the last five weeks, and its quantity was part of its charm. She felt lost in a sea of food: creamed potatoes lapped at her elbows, in the far distance was a clump of roast parsnips she was looking forward to sampling after the carrots, beans, and pineapple fritters, and it was reassuring to know that this delightful experience was going to last for most of the foreseeable future. She could see why Pug refused to eat anything down at the farm; if you fed like this four times a day it would probably kill you to top up with a snack.

At the start of the meal Sherry had leaned over to cut up Jack's meat, her breasts almost bobbling out of the top of her dress, and while he ate she kept shifting on her seat, pressing herself against him in a crackle of static. Kitty didn't need to watch to be acutely aware of what was going on on the other side of the table, it was as if it was all happening inside her own skull, muffled by an incoming tide of parsley sauce.

After about twenty minutes her attitude to the meal altered, and it became an exquisite torture, still delicious, but more and more impossible to get down. There was a bad moment when a good half-pound of mashed potato, silky with butter, began fighting its way back up her throat and had to be persuaded down again with a jugful of lemonade shandy, and it was reassuring when the men showed signs of the same difficulty: putting their forks down to discuss market prices, and patting their belts. They all made it, though, and Kitty was looking proudly round at their empty plates when Sherry reappeared from the kitchen with a cylindrical steamed sultana sponge and a bucket of clotted cream.

In Kitty's university town there was a restaurant with an unusual gimmick. It specialised in steak-and-kidney pudding and a light, fluffy cheesecake, and pinned to one wall was the offer of a refund to anyone who could eat three successive helpings of both. Few impoverished students could resist such a challenge, and Kitty knew plenty who'd starved themselves before taking it up. Others had sworn by a training regime that gradually accustomed the stomach to greater quantities, and her tutorial partner claimed he'd only failed because he foolishly missed out on an egg and bacon breakfast the morning of his attempt. Kitty didn't actually know anyone who'd succeeded – she'd only ever seen defeated contenders, all looking strangely

116

similar, their jaw-lines puffy as they stared at half a cheesecake with glazed horror. Now she knew exactly how they'd felt.

She stayed behind to help Sherry with the washing-up, glad to defer her next meeting with Geoff Jiggins. Sherry tidied the dinner dishes onto a tray and gave the saloon bar a careful look. The tables needed an extra gloss of polish, and the fire another shovelful of coal.

"Those two old bats of yours are coming in soon," she said. "It has to be right."

"Surely it doesn't matter that much what the place looks like, providing some effort's been made," Kitty said, holding the swing doors open.

"That's where you're wrong. It's the little bit extra on top that's the most important. That's why you'll have a hard time down at Balls' unless there's been a fair bit of spring-cleaning since I saw it last. If a room's clean enough it keeps the guests in order. They don't hardly dare breathe, and that's how you want them. They'll mess you about if they feel at home."

The kitchen was a narrow room crammed with electrical gadgets, its walls sweaty with condensation, and every conceivable surface was heaped with dirty dishes and pots. Sherry laughed at Kitty's expression of dismay. "Don't worry about this mess," she said. "I don't! Health inspector isn't due for another couple of weeks, and as far as I'm concerned it can stay there."

A two-tone chime went, and she swiftly opened the cupboards and freezers, cramming eight scones and a teapot into a microwave.

"Here," she said. "If you want to be useful you can stuff some of that in there." She vanished through the flap door and Kitty found herself holding a glass jamjar, so clean it flashed like a diamond, and a familiar rusty bollard of a tin, labelled 'Red Jam'.

The tea tray looked faultless when Sherry had finished with it. The jam was topped with a ribboned gingham cover, curls of butter hung round a dish of cream and four big wedges of cream cake were piled below the scones on a glass stand.

"The secret of cooking, as far as I can see," said Sherry, as she eased open the door with a hip, "is making it look good and giving them too much to eat. They'll pay anything for that."

When she got back she poured Kitty a cup of black coffee and offered her a cigarette. "Pug tells me they're permanents from the Social. How're you getting on?"

"Not too bad. It's a funny system, though. I wouldn't want to be stuck with the same guests for years and years."

"I would! You only have to change the beds once a fortnight if you're sharp about it, there's no fuss with bookings, and the money's good: two hundred quid a week."

"I didn't know it was that much." For a moment Kitty was almost shocked at the profit Roger was making. It was strange to think of the old ladies as financial assets that could inspire envy. She changed the subject. "We've got an ordinary holiday-maker in today. He seems rather peculiar, and what really worries me is I can't see how I'm going to stop him hanging round the kitchen all day."

"Well, that's not very difficult is it? Just tell him he's got to go out, it isn't convenient to have him indoors."

"Supposing he says no?"

"It never happens."

"It might to me."

Sherry blew smoke at Kitty. "You could have a point there. You don't look right: you're too young, and you're much too small – you need presence for this game; you got to be able to scare the wits out of them with a look. I had a family in yesterday for bed and breakfast, and when I went to the bathroom I found one of them had chucked up in the basin, blocked it right up with sick. I hate sick, you get enough of it in the gents. Anyway, there they all were in the saloon; four of them: two adults and two teenagers, old enough to know better. They were waiting for their breakfast, wanted boiled eggs just to be difficult, and I went in and said 'You're not getting your boiled eggs, and you're not leaving, neither, till that sick's cleared.' And I gave them my look." Sherry narrowed her eyes, and her mouth shrivelled to a slit, remembering. "It didn't take long. Couple of minutes, I'd say, before the father, big strong sort, too, made a choking noise and hurried out the room."

"But surely people won't come back if you treat them that way?"

"Who wants people like that to come back? Not me."

The hard, embittered look faded from Sherry's face, and she smiled, so Kitty felt encouraged to insist: "But you do have to give good service, don't you? Make them feel happy, that sort of thing?"

"Oh yes – any minute now I'm going to have to throw you out so I can give those two old bags their money's worth on dog-breeding; it's part of the job, chatting people up, and smiling till your cheeks ache – but that's got nothing to do with being soft. No one likes you for being soft. That's where Deb was so good: she made them feel like they were staying with their favourite auntie. Best behaviour all round. Terrible cook, she was – a free hand with the tin-opener and the hundreds and thousands – but she was packing them in."

"What was she like as a person?" Sherry glanced sideways, and wiped a smear of gravy off the top of the freezer. Her face looked almost beautiful, in a strong-jawed, Edwardian way, when she was thinking. She'd certainly taken great pains with her head: her skin was lightly and skilfully made up, and her hair streaked blonde and permed into loose curls.

"She was never satisfied with what she'd got," she

said. "Always felt hard done by and wanted someone else's share, and didn't care too much what they thought about it. She was smart and bright; I liked her. When Puggie first brung me out here, she was the only one who was friendly. But then there was a good reason for that."

"What reason?"

Sherry looked at her with astonishment. "Didn't you know? She was after Puggie, wasn't she?"

"After Pug?" Kitty found it impossible to keep an insulting note of disbelief from her voice.

"Well, he's a good-looking man," Sherry said defensively. Kitty swallowed and nodded. "I have to watch him even now; blacked his eye for him the other night when he came in late. He won't be taking another evening off in a hurry. It's no use looking at me like that. If you want to keep Jack you're going to have to do the same."

After putting Sherry straight about her non-relationship with Jack, Kitty ran down the hill to the farm, exhilarated by her own snappily angry sentences. Her life seemed simple again, and only a matter of modifying her behaviour in the easiest possible way. If Sherry could keep guests in order, so could she – she only had to summon a little courage, and she'd never been short of that.

"I'm very sorry, but we don't have the facilities for you to stay here during the day," she said sternly to a bunch of ewes sheltering under the hedge, and she practised yelling, "You've got to go OUT, Mrs Ridley," at a whirling mass of lambs leaping and skipping their way up the field. The echo was very satisfying, and she was seeing how loud she could get it when she spotted a familiar brace of raspberry anoraks breasting the rise of the hill, and bolted for the safety of the yard.

Once there, she thought she'd see if she could get

another handful of Deborah May's letters. She walked quietly into the inner yard and crouched at the entrance to the kennel. It was empty. The inside looked far less attractive in daylight: the floor was sprinkled with squishy green droppings, and the nest in the centre held stained paper and feathers grey with dirt. She crept right inside and riffled through. There were a few envelopes addressed to a Mrs H. Banty in Ontario, Canada, but the remaining bits of letter were only scraps, too torn to be legible.

There was a hard lump in the middle of the nest. She dug down and pulled out an enormous egg, very clean and white. Where it had been sitting was a triangle of blue: a folded sheet of paper half-buried in the earth floor. It was the first page of a letter, and as she smoothed it out she heard a soft, croaking, cackling sound, the kind of noise the geese made as they roved from one appointment to another. They were lovers of routine, and she knew their timetable intimately. It went:

7 a.m. to 8.15 shriek under bedroom windows
8.15 clean out drains outside the kitchen
8.19 rush across the yard on tiptoe, wings flapping and necks outstretched
8.20 to 8.40 wipe beaks on washing hanging on the line, pull down towels if possible, and crap on them
8.41 waddle slowly past back door, honk menacingly at dog
and so on.

According to this schedule they ought to be far out across the meadow now, grazing beside Blossom. She turned round with difficulty, scraping her elbow on the brickwork, and looked out. A white head was peering in at her, one eye glassily enlarged. It cogitated, marshalling all the facts in the case, before opening its beak, so she could see a pointed orange tongue, and letting out a hiss.

Then it withdrew, and there was a scuffle outside and the sound of low goose voices conferring. Kitty waited in the kennel. Something tickled her left hand where it was resting on the ground and she looked down and saw a black-beetle lying playfully on its back, tweaking at the heel of her palm with its pincers. She brushed it away, and the gander slapped into view, turned with a proud flutter of white, and stared at her. He had an odd face: however long you studied it you couldn't see an expression. It was like a nostril or an eyebrow, it didn't mean anything on its own; to determine what the gander was thinking you had to look at his whole body, the alignment of his wings and the placing of his neck and feet. He seemed, from what she could judge, to be torn between aggression and wariness. It probably wasn't very often that he found a human crouching in his kennel. Maybe he didn't even know she was a human. It could just be her face, floating threateningly above his precious egg, that disturbed him.

He pondered the situation, flapping his webs on the concrete, and Kitty sensed he could easily go on the same way for hours. She had to get back and start the tea, and since she'd always been the kind of person to get nasty, painful moments over as quickly as possible, she tensed, raised herself on her feet and hands, and made a sudden rush from the kennel on all fours. The gander gave a shriek of surprise, and only recovered himself as she was straightening up, catching her an agonizing blow on the bridge of the nose with his wing. As she ran out of the yard, clutching her nose, pursued by flailing white wings, she saw Mr Jiggins watching her.

"I wondered where you'd got to!" he said. "Do you often play with the geese?"

"Yes, it's lovely," she said, leaping for the safety of the dog's room. "Why don't you try it some time?" Privately she swore a deep and terrible oath: never

122

never never was she going near the goose nest again. Deborah May's letters simply weren't worth such pain.

Dear Hilda,
I am in trouble and I can not go on living here any longer. If you would only loan me the money I would come out to you with Jack. You must reply to me this time.

On Thursday last week it was Jack's birthday. He was ten years old and I took him out of school for a treat and did not let Rog make him work, and we went down by the river. I had no money to buy him a present, Rog keeps me so short, but I made a cake and we had a picnic.

About five in the evening I saw a van and trailer draw up in the yard and Philip came to the door and asked for Jack.

He looked coldly at her. "Where is he? The boy?"

"Why? What do you want him for?" She could see he didn't like having to talk to her.

"I want him, isn't that enough?"

Jack heard his voice, ran out from the kitchen and jumped into his arms. "I've a present for you," Philip said. "You want to see it?"

Jack squealed with excitement, and Philip held him, wriggling, above his head and carried him out into the yard. Deborah followed, feeling that was all she was on this farm, a shadow that kept behind the men. She loved Jack, but she hated the way he meant more than she did. If by chance she and Jack spoke at the same time, he was the one the men wanted to hear, she was the one had to be silent.

Philip set Jack down by the trailer and Deborah heard Rog's tractor change gear out across the fields; he'd be back for his tea soon. Philip spun the fastening nuts on the trailer tailgate, and it dropped with a creak, showing a pale movement behind inner gates.

"What is it, Mum?" Jack was so excited he couldn't keep still, he ran round the ramp, his Wellingtons rattling.

"Keep back!" Philip fended him off, then opened the gates and ducked inside. There was a rattle of chain before he led out a smoky-grey foal. It whinnied with fear and tried to escape back into the trailer, but he wrapped his arms round its neck and rump, and pushed it, stiff-legged, down the ramp.

"Take a good look," he said to Jack. "She's yours now. A carthorse filly. She'll be pure white when she's grown."

"You're never giving him that? You can't, Philip, you can't do that to Rog." She'd always thought she hated Rog, but now she realised she must care for him after all, if she wanted so desperately to stop him being hurt.

"Why shouldn't I give him the filly? What's to stop me giving my own son a birthday present?"

In answer, Roger's tractor came jolting down the drive.

10

The next day it began to snow in a dedicated manner, soft flakes that didn't wink out into puddles when they landed, but settled into thick ripples across the concrete. That evening, Kitty's awareness of Jack was electric. He and Roger were discussing the frozen pipes in the milking parlour, and though she kept her head down and tried to concentrate on her meal she was aware of every breath he took, and every gesture he made. He'd taken off his sling and hidden his injured hand inside an old sock, and she could hear it rustling; once a crystal of snow flicked off the wool and landed beside her plate. She couldn't get over how strong he looked, and how healthy. His face glowed from the cold and he was wearing a beautiful sweater, faded powder blue with careful darns all over it, which made him look childish and vulnerable. She'd never asked his age, just assumed he was in his early twenties, but now it occurred to her that he could be much younger.

"If there's drifting, the milk'll have to go across the fields. Roads'll be out."

"Is it going to get that bad?" Kitty couldn't help interrupting.

Jack looked at her and his lips curled in a smile. It wasn't a very pleasant smile – it seemed to imply that he knew all about her and had a definite plan for what he was going to do with her, which he'd get round to

125

when he wasn't so busy – but though she disliked it Kitty couldn't help tingling with excitement. "We could be snowed up for days," he said. "Weeks, even. I've been expecting this for over a month, I'm surprised it didn't come sooner."

"It were too cold to snow, up till now," Roger added sagely.

As usual, Geoff Jiggins bobbed into the kitchen when the men had gone. After only a day and a half of his company Kitty felt haunted: she couldn't be alone for an instant without him appearing at her side, an anxious, tearful expression on his face. If only she was like Sherry, how simple it would be to get rid of him! But she didn't want to hurt his feelings, and also, she was ashamed to admit, she wanted him to like her. She wanted everyone to like her.

Pleasing Mr Jiggins was no easy matter. Her friendliness had given him confidence: he encouraged her to talk about herself, and when she responded a patronising smile would flicker across his face. She felt exhausted after their conversations, as if a vampire had been feeding off her. There was more than a suspicion of vampire about Mr Jiggins. His teeth were unusually small and even, and when he smiled he looked slightly vicious, reminding Kitty of the kind of predator that creeps up behind its prey and catches it at a disadvantage.

The only way to escape him was to go and visit Lancelot. She was reluctant to, even though it was the lamb's feeding-time, because Jack was often in the lambing shed and she didn't want to encourage him. She needed time to think about her feelings before making a new commitment. On the other hand, she definitely couldn't take any more of Mr Jiggins.

The wind filled her coat with snow and blew her across the yard. It was banging on the roof of the lambing shed and rattling the hinges of the metal door, but Lancelot still heard and recognised her step. He gave a nasal jabber and flailed at the sides of his pen, and she eased him out over the top. He was too big to sit on her lap now, he'd grown astonishingly gross and meaty, and his stomach was almost spherical, like a woollen balloon. Sometimes she worried about all the trapped wind in there and imagined him exploding with a muffled boom. It wasn't her fault, she'd done her best to stop him swallowing air, but he was such an aggressive feeder. He'd suck so hard the teat would pop off the bottle and catch in his throat, and then he'd frisk away from her grasp, making a high whistling noise and visibly swelling with air. He didn't do that this evening, he drank carefully, yawned so a tiny ripple of fat ran up his back and prinked his tail, and settled his head on her knee.

It was cold in the shed. The light was swinging wildly on its cord, and all the ewes and lambs from the fields were crammed in at the far end, their wool dark with moisture and the straw beneath their feet trampled and soiled. They shifted restlessly, frightened, and Kitty caught their mood and began to worry about the other animals on the farm. Were they all protected from the snow? What about the horses? It suddenly seemed vitally important to find out, so she carried Lancelot back to his pen, where he settled with a dreamy sigh, and looked outside. The sky had gone a deep lead colour, and snow was falling faster and faster. It was slanting towards the old, inner yard, and she pulled her coat up over her head and ran blindly round to the stable. The door was banging open in the wind, but she knew, before she even crossed the threshold, that there was a horse in there. She could feel its warm breath. She fumbled for a light switch and a bulb snapped on, its surface dim with fly-speckles. Blossom's grubby white head looked at her over the top of the end stall with a humorous expression. Kitty tiptoed a little closer. She distinctly remembered Jack telling her that this mare didn't like stables – had indeed been put off going in them permanently through Kitty's stupidity. Why then, was she here?

The door banged again behind her, a mournful, neglected sound. The stable looked neglected too, the stalls bare and swept clean. Kitty pulled herself up on the wooden divider and peered into Blossom's manger. It was completely empty. There was even a big web across one corner, which had clearly taken several hours' effort on the part of some spider. Blossom dipped her head and huffed at the empty manger. Jack didn't know she was in here, then. He couldn't, or he would have given her something to eat. Well, Kitty could soon put that right.

There was a stack of four bales by the door: two very pale green with fine stalks, the others much yellower and coarser, so it seemed reasonable to assume the green ones were hay. She'd always thought it was yellow; maybe this was a special connoisseur's variety: the equine equivalent of Lance's Lebanese Gold hashish. The trouble was, someone had strapped the bale up ridiculously tightly with hairy orange string. She couldn't pull it off, it was embedded like a belt in a fat waist, so she tried gnawing instead, but that didn't work either. Finally, in desperation, she picked it up, and the string broke at once. She threw the hay at Blossom over the divider, not wanting to get too close to her, and it was so satisfying watching her eat that she thought she'd try lobbing her some straw to sleep on. The string on the straw bales appeared to have been put there by a crazed caterpillar, they were almost totally cocooned in the stuff, and it took a little time to work a handful out. When it was free she stood well back and chucked it at the pool of darkness by Blossom's back feet. Blossom turned, as if sizing up Kitty's potential as a threat, and the patch of darkness caught the light and rippled like silk.

"Wait there! Don't move!" Kitty shouted, and raced outside. The buildings were only smoky outlines now, behind frantic whiteness. "Jack!" she called, and snow blew into her mouth. She ran into the concrete yard. The sheep looked as mournful as ever, and she could see Geoff Jiggins's spooky silhouette outlined in the kitchen window. He was doing something in the sink, and he raised his head and looked out at her. She ducked back into the inner yard. Jack's chicken house was somewhere back here. She was trying to identify the clump of saplings she'd seen near it when she bumped into something solid, and Jack caught her firmly round the shoulders.

"What are you doing?" he asked, his voice as teasingly affectionate as it was when he talked to his mare. "Were you looking for me?"

Kitty quivered at his touch. "It's Blossom," she cried.

"What do you want with Blossom, hey? She's all right. She's out under the hedge. I saw her back along. Horses don't mind the snow; it's the wet they hates."

"She's in the stable now. And I think – I'm pretty sure – she's had a foal."

Jack let her go and disappeared into the snow, and very slowly, taking pains to avoid the young trees and random blocks of stone that littered this part of the farm, Kitty followed. She wished she hadn't told him about Blossom now, it had been so lovely when he was holding her. Who was she kidding? That was what she wanted more than anything, to be kissed and maybe loved. It had been a long time since she last saw Lance. She even had difficulty now remembering what he looked like. His face seemed to have merged oddly with Lancelot the lamb's, so when she tried to conjure up those fine, bony features they kept being topped by pointy ears and covered in wool.

When she reached the stable Jack was crouched

beside the foal, coaxing it to its feet. It seemed frail and its coat was wet with moisture.

"He hasn't been born long," he said. "Was she down and straining when you come in?"

"No." Kitty sat on the last two remaining bales and watched him. "She was standing up, looking hungry. That's why I gave her some hay." She wished Jack would congratulate her. She thought it an extraordinary feat of initiative and bravery to have fed Blossom.

"I've always wanted to see a foal born," Jack said. "And I've never managed it. They say the foal comes out with a pad on his tongue, like a slice of liver, and if you snatch it off and keep it you can charm any horse, even a wild stallion. I could do with one of them for that Truncheon."

"Is that really true?"

"O yes, I even seen one. A veterinary come in once, up Pug's, and he was showing it around. It looked like a bit of wrinkled-up shoe-leather." He sucked in a breath. "It may be a load of cobblers but I'd still like one." He put his arms round the foal's body and pulled it upright. It was enormous, for a baby: its head came up to his shoulder. "Are you going to try for a drink?" he asked it. "It's here, look." He tweaked something that also resembled a bit of wrinkled-up shoe-leather, hanging near Blossom's back legs. A thin jet of milk came out, and with great gentleness he guided the foal's lips towards it; throughout all this Blossom ate, occasionally casting an indulgent glance at the two of them. When the foal was sucking Jack picked up the bale of straw Kitty had dropped, and undid it, muttering something angry about a baler. He'd begun shaking the sections out when he stopped and kicked them aside with his boot.

"What is it?" Kitty asked.

"Nothing. Just I expected to see her afterbirth, and it

isn't there. You didn't see it earlier, did you? When you was here?"

"I don't think so. What does it look like?"

"You couldn't miss it; it's like a big pancake, and dark red. Only sometimes they eat it, see. It's good for them."

"So perhaps she's eaten it. What does it matter?"

"If she hasn't, and it's still inside her, that's serious."

"How serious?" Kitty got to her feet and began looking for anything that resembled a gigantic red pancake. There seemed to be a lot of unpleasant things that dropped off or fell out of carthorses. She wasn't sure she wanted to be the one to find the afterbirth. She kicked a lump of straw aside and shuddered when she saw something glint, but it was only some water Blossom had passed. Jack didn't answer her question.

"Foal's sucking well; that'll make it come out," he said hopefully, and settled down for a long wait, pushing up the collar of his jacket.

The telephone pinged at midnight. Kitty was only half-asleep, she'd been listening to the wind roaring outside the house and the ivy rustling in the snow. Jack's voice rose and fell in the room below; he seemed to have the same careless attitude to sleeping guests as his father. When she'd dressed in the dark and crept down into the hall she saw light and shadow wavering out from the open door of the lounge.

"What I'm afraid of," he was saying, "is not getting it all. I'm willing to have a try but I don't know what I'm doing. Now, if I gets it to you, will you look at it and tell me if it's whole? Because that's what scares me. Scares me rigid, it do."

He was perched on an arm of the sofa, a hurricane lamp smoking at his feet. Its light cut deep lines in his face, making his eyes intent and almost predatory, like a hawk's. He winked at Kitty while he was talking and soon put the telephone down.

"I was thinking of coming to get you," he said. "I could do with a hand with Blossom." He led the way round through the kitchen to the dog's room, and insisted on dressing her in a waxed cotton coat hanging behind the door. (She saw one eye flash in the semi-dark as the dog decided to himself that it wasn't worth getting up.)

"It's evil out there," Jack said, buttoning Kitty up so she felt like a child being dressed for an outing.

"What's happening to Blossom?"

He pulled the hood over her head and stood back to consider the effect. "You'll need a scarf." He picked an unappetisingly crispy one off the dog's bed. "She's lively, but she hasn't cleansed yet. I got to get it out now meself." When she was dressed to his satisfaction – she felt ludicrous, her sleeves touched the tops of her rubber boots – he took her hand in his unhurt one and opened the door.

In the army camp where she'd worked there'd been a potato-peeling machine, and the first time she'd used it she'd left it on too long, so when she looked through the glass porthole she'd seen hundreds of peanut-sized potatoes dancing at high velocity, like a swarm of angry bees. The memory came to mind now as Jack pulled her into the yard, because the experience was like stepping into that potato-peeler. Sharp pieces of snow scoured her face, she could see nothing except her own tears, and the wind pushed her and screamed in her ears.

"Don't let go," Jack shouted, as they turned the corner of the stable and the blizzard lifted her off her feet. She held tighter to his hand, and didn't release it until the stable door was shut behind them. It was indescribably warm and snug in there. Blossom was cropping at her hay, and the foal was curled up in an

132

angular bundle, his long, veined head resting on folded legs.

"What can I do to help?" Kitty asked, watching a cone of snow build up beside a crack in the door.

Jack slapped his arms to knock the snow off. "Go up the top end and hold her head. Try and keep her still as you can."

Kitty swallowed. It meant squeezing along the wall, past Blossom's horribly dangerous back legs, but she couldn't let Jack down. The mare had a half-smile on her floppy lips when Kitty reached them, and she dipped her head and huffed down the front of Kitty's coat.

"Catch hold of her halter and hold her steady," Jack called.

Blossom evidently saw Kitty as an amusing toy, placed in front of the manger to provide a little light relief, and she whiffled into her ears, slobbered on the end of her nose, and champed on one of the toggles of her coat. She was gentle but determined, and she didn't seem at all bothered by what Jack was doing at her other end. Every so often, as the mare's head dipped, Kitty got a partial view of Jack. He rolled his sleeves up past the elbow and pressed himself close against the horse, so for a while all that was visible were a few of his black curls against the yellowy-white rump.

Then Blossom stiffened; the whites of her eyes showed and her nostrils flared as if she was catching a terrifying scent. Kitty took a firmer hold on the bridle: she could feel the mare's muscles tensing, and sensed she was about to move. Hooves clicked on the stone floor and Jack stepped backwards into view. There was a wet rustling, and a red rope appeared at the end of his hand. He was winding it steadily out of Blossom and his action reminded Kitty of a cook stretching strudel pastry; there didn't seem a lot of effort involved, just skill, patience, and the right tension. The rope flapped and Blossom relaxed, her eyes going soft. Kitty released her and she began feeding again.

"Good," Jack murmured. "She wasn't any trouble?"

"No, she was fine." Kitty crept back along the wall, anxious to avoid annoying Blossom by going too near her foal. "I don't think you really needed me," she added, but Jack wasn't listening, he was untwisting the rope and spreading it out in an empty stall. It looked like a pair of tights when it was smoothed, a macabre pair, dull blood-coloured, with pink and purple highlights. The feet were frayed into toes; Jack crouched down and pulled them out.

"See, I can't tell if I've got it all or no. There could be a piece missing off one of these ends."

"Would that matter?"

"If there's a fraction left inside it'll go septic and kill her."

"What are you going to do, then?"

"I'm taking the whole lot to the veterinary; he's not far, only ten mile outside Wormington." Jack rolled the afterbirth into a disagreeable-looking sausage and stuffed it into his pocket.

"You can't go now, not when it's like that outside! You'll freeze to death or get lost. Can't you wait until it gets a bit calmer?"

"No. She has to be clear of her cleansing eight hours after the birth, and we've had five of them already. I can't afford to wait; but don't you throw a wobbly about me and the snow, I've lived here all my life. I know this valley, and it'll take more than bad weather to kill me off."

11

When morning came the windows were luminous with snow. There wasn't a sound from outside; the wind had died. Downstairs there were oily streaks on the wallpaper where Jack's lamp had passed, and the back door was open. Roger's squat black footprints had smashed through the deep drifts arcing across the yard. He'd visited every doorway, pattering backwards and forwards like a mouse dancing round a piece of cheese. She could only see his prints, and the reluctant pads left by the dog; nothing that was Jack's.

Blossom stood, head drooping, in the dusty stable, and Kitty waded through a drift that came up to her waist until she came to the little chicken house among the saplings. There was no smoke blowing out of the pipe in the roof today. She turned the doorknob, and as she did so heard the farmhouse generator start up with a clanking rattle.

The hinge was a little stiff, but gave inwards, with a push, and she was surprised by what she found inside. The air was cold, and mustily sweet, but what she noticed first was the enormous furniture. A heavy wardrobe tipped forwards on her left, a television set balanced on one open drawer, and facing it was a brass double bed. Behind them a roll-top desk curved up to the ceiling, with a stuffed fox balanced on top. The room was so tiny that only a narrow strip of floor was left to walk on; Kitty wobbled along it and sat down on the bed. She could see now that there was a stone sink on one side of the door, and a home-made metal stove on the other. A string ran across the corner above the stove with two pairs of socks drying on it. It was odd, but this room had about it the exact flavour of the country she'd been seeking when she first applied for a job at Balls Farm. There was a rough cosiness to the wallpaper – a mottled brown that reminded her of a cigar box she'd been given as a little girl, to store treasures in – and a sweet dignity to the furniture: the same rich chestnut inlaid with gold that she'd seen in the loft above the stable. What most impressed her was the room's neatness. The bed even had fresh sheets on it, unironed but very white, and down beside it was a bottle of whisky with the seal unbroken. She leaned over for a better look. The bottle of whisky was on a tray, along with a new bottle of ginger ale – she frowned, that seemed untypical of Jack somehow – and two unused glasses.

She giggled. All it needed was a pink-shaded lamp and some romantic music and it couldn't have been a more obvious setting for a seduction. It was touching that Jack had gone to all this trouble on her behalf; it made him seem less alarmingly strong and self-confident. As she stole out and shut the door behind her, she wished she could rub out the footprints in the snow that showed so clearly where she'd been. Maybe she could scrubble them about with the end of a branch, the way Indians did in Westerns. Of course there wasn't a suitable fallen branch to hand, so Kitty jumped about all over her footprints instead, making it look as if a crowd of dwarfs in size 5 Wellington boots had pressed round the door of the chicken house before stampeding *en masse* back to the farm.

She couldn't concentrate on making breakfast: she kept thinking of Jack, and the way he'd said, "It'll take more than bad weather to kill me off", before going out into the blizzard. She was in no mood for fussing over whether her fried tomatoes had achieved the correct balance between liquidity and firmness. (Who'd invented cooked breakfasts, anyway, with all those ingredients that had to be cooked in the same fat at varying temperatures? Probably the same English sadist who'd devised Sunday roasts, a thinly disguised ruse to ensure that half the nation spent Sunday afternoon scraping bits of Yorkshire pudding off non-stick patty pans.) She made scrambled eggs instead, and they didn't go down well in the dining room. The two ladies had their anoraks on in protest against the cold, and when she put the tray down Geoff Jiggins said: "What unusual food you serve here!"

"Whatever it is, it's undercooked," Mayonne sniffed, poking at it with her fork.

Miss Biffen suggested that it might be a pleasant surprise, but she didn't sound convinced. She cocked her head and bared her lips as she lifted the first forkful. She always did that before she ate anything, but it was still interesting to watch, however many times you saw it.

Roger had been in twice, muttering to himself about Jack's absence and smearing slush over the linoleum, before a dark shadow fluttered across the white glaze on the kitchen window. Kitty dropped her dishcloth and ran round to the dog's room, scarcely daring to breathe in case it wasn't Jack after all. But it was. He dipped his head to get in and leaned back against the wall with his hands in his pockets. Snow crusted his clothes up to mid-thigh, but the rest of him seemed unaffected: his hair was dry and almost fluffy, and his cheeks only a little reddened by the wind. For an instant she thought he was an illusion, he looked so different from what she'd expected, so much fitter and bigger. When she thought about him she never seemed able to conjure up his solidity and vitality; each time she saw it she was surprised.

"Ask me how I got on, then," he said, finding it impossible not to smile.

"How did you?"

"It wasn't too great getting up the valley; I had to do most of it on me hands and knees, but it was a piece of piss once I was up top. I shook Pug out of bed and got him to start his van – it's an old Morris Minor, and a load of concrete in the back keeps it from slipping on the snow. Pug tried to leg it back to the pub a couple of times, but once we got going he was no trouble. Scares easy, Pug do."

"What about the afterbirth?"

"That's all sorted. Veterinary told me it were all out, said he couldn't have done a better job his self – well, I've watched him often enough, Blossom's always been slow to cleanse. You'd like him, he talks like you. Ill-looking bloke, and thin as a rasher of wind, but I've never seen as many books as he has up there. He's got all these framed certificates too, real educated." He shook a loose curl out of his eyes. "How's Blossom?"

"She's well." Kitty's voice was thoughtful; she felt it wouldn't be accurate to be more enthusiastic. There'd been a sad, tired look about the mare this morning, and even her foal had seemed depressed.

Jack considered her, his eyelashes very dark against his skin. "It takes it out of them, foaling," he said. "And she had me messing about, too. I'll give her some grub, that'll liven her up."

"Where did you sleep?" Kitty asked suddenly, and then blushed, for some unknown reason.

"Up at Pug's. They're doing well there, packing them in three to a room; plonkers that got stuck on the main road. I slept in the public – with me head under the beer tap."

There was a bang from the milking parlour, and an obscene curse.

"Old man's temper isn't any sweeter," Jack observed, before ducking back outside. Kitty watched him pick his way through the snow towards the stable, and admired the grace of his movements. Funny to think she'd once found his swagger irritating.

Later, as she was dusting Geoff Jiggins's room, she saw Roger and Jack climb on the tractor and drive off across the fields, a huge blue plastic container of milk wobbling on the trailer behind them. The wheels stuck and revved on the snow every so often, leaving two deep parallel tracks; not just slush, but torn earth as well. She was disappointed they hadn't left her any instructions for looking after the animals; after all, she had been left in sole charge of the farm. She decided to startle them with her competence and efficiency. In fact, she rather hoped there'd be an emergency for her to deal with.

Geoff's room was interesting to dust. There was a paperback about the occult beside the bed, and next to it a Bible with a special magazine tucked inside, giving a mini-sermon for each day. On the back cover of this worthy journal a terrible job was advertised: working in a vegetarian café in exchange for rent-free caravan accommodation and as many wholefood leftovers as you could eat. Kitty gloated over it for a while before moving on to the dressing table. Geoff had the largest collection of cosmetics she'd ever seen, and placed incongruously in their midst was a small watering can. It seemed to be well-used; she'd checked on it a number of times today, and on each occasion it had been in a different position, sometimes half-full of murky water, sometimes empty. She longed to know what it was for, but that wasn't the kind of question you could ask: the things you saw in other people's rooms were like confessional secrets.

139

As she came out on the landing she heard a peculiar sound from downstairs, and her first thought was that one of the guests was having a heart attack, but as she got closer she recognised it as laughter. Looking through the dining room keyhole she saw Miss Biffen clasping a fan of playing cards to her cardigan, a delighted, naughty look on her face. Geoff was wagging a finger at her and saying, "No you don't!" And though Mrs Ridley was facing the other way Kitty thought the back of her head looked indulgent rather than disapproving.

In the afternoon all three of them went up to look at the drifts on the main road. Kitty heard their voices as they went past the hall window, and saw their colourful figures struggling up the long white sweep of drive: the two ladies brilliant raspberry and Geoff Jiggins a dull, smoky green. She watched them wistfully, feeling lonely and excluded from the fun. It seemed to her that for far too long she'd been an onlooker, spying on others and never having any enjoyment she could truly call her own. She hesitated by the back door; she didn't like any of the guests that much, but they did seem happy: she heard an excited shout and saw snowballs flying. On impulse she plunged after them up the drive, and she was half-way up when a shrill noise began behind her. It sounded like a pig with a clear treble voice, backed by a chorus of grunts and snortles.

She turned back, angry with herself for being reluctant. This could be an emergency that needed her swift intervention; she owed it to the Snells to behave responsibly towards their animals. As she slipped and slid into the yard she saw something dirty white moving beside the blockhouse where the pigs were kept. It twisted and flapped against the dazzling snow, and when she got closer she saw it was a pig's head; not dead, but very much alive. The mouth was wide open, showing pearly teeth and a fresh red tongue, and it was making the most piercing sound she'd ever heard, a jabbering scream that sliced into her brain like a razor-blade.

She crouched down in the snow and put her hand on the animal's hot ear. There was a blissful millisecond of peace while it jerked with shock and swivelled round to look at her, then its pupils dilated, its mouth opened, and the noise began again, even worse than before. Kitty couldn't work out what had happened at first – the situation resembled a still from a horror film or a detail from a painting by Hieronymus Bosch – but then she felt the pig's neck and discovered it was wedged in a drain-hole. The animal must have pushed itself through from the blockhouse, and if it had managed that, it must be possible to stuff it back in again. She grabbed its head and pushed. The screaming became higher and thinner, but the head didn't disappear; the ears just flushed magenta. Kitty slid the bolts on the pig-house and looked inside, with the idea of pulling the pig through from the other side. It was extremely hot in there, and smelt horrible, and when the latch dropped back on itself with a click every pig in the place – and there seemed to be millions – began squealing. She shut the door hastily, but the noise didn't stop, it got more frenzied.

In desperation she seized on the idea of food. Pigs were greedy, weren't they? Maybe if she gave the head a snack it would stop making such an intolerable noise. She mixed up a bowl of muesli, and on her way out of the kitchen saw a balaclava helmet lying on the floor. That might be useful: being cold made anyone bad-tempered, and if the pig's ears were warm it would probably calm down. She was wrong: the animal seemed to resent the balaclava: it snapped ungraciously as the ribbing was eased over its head, and certainly looked most peculiar when it was on.

"Be quiet!" Kitty said severely, scraping the extra off

the side of the spoon, the way she'd seen mothers do when they were feeding toddlers. But the pig wasn't interested in muesli, it just squealed more and more desperately, and its panic began to affect her. If only Jack would come back! "Please come back," she muttered, bent over and hugging herself in the snow, as the pig, looking like an enraged baby, shrilled in its bonnet before her.

"You're bloody mad, you are," Jack laughed, when he returned at nightfall. He and Roger freed the pig easily, one holding the head and the other going into the blockhouse and manoeuvring the body which the rest of the pigs were snapping at in the most heartless manner. Kitty had had an agonising afternoon. She'd been forced to go indoors and start cooking at four o'clock, and it had been terrible looking out of the window and seeing that brown, knitted head wailing to itself in the falling snow.

Jack hurried over his food and got up, wiping his mouth on his sleeve. "I'm going to look at the mare," he said, turning to pull his coat off the back of his chair. "You coming?"

Kitty saw Roger gaze at him open-mouthed, and when she was outside realised why. It was the first time he'd ever heard Jack speaking to her. She rather expected Jack to take her hand or put his arm over her shoulders, but he didn't. He walked ahead, whistling to himself, and she was expected to keep a few respectful paces behind, like a goose following a gander.

Blossom's head wasn't looking over the wooden divider when Kitty got to the stable, and Jack had disappeared too. She ran up to the end stall and found them both on the floor. Blossom propped up on folded front legs while Jack stroked her mane slowly and tenderly.

142

"She's not right," he said.

"Isn't she just tired?"

"No; she's hurt inside, I can feel it. She wouldn't be down like this else."

Kitty sat shyly against the wall and watched him. He murmured so quietly to the mare that she couldn't catch his words, but they had an effect, because Blossom suddenly made a convulsive attempt to get to her feet. She couldn't make it; her huge body, so comically graceful when it was upright, seemed too heavy for her now. Jack gripped her bridle and urged her: "Come on now, Blossom." He clicked his tongue. "You can do it. Hup hup hup." Her legs banged against the wooden stall-divider, and her foal trembled beside her, crest taut and nostrils flaring, like a rocking horse. Blossom was about to push herself upright when she gave up and collapsed back on the straw, breathing heavily, and Kitty noticed how flat and damp her coat was, where she'd been lying on it earlier.

"I've got to get her to her feet," Jack said. "Stay here and watch her; I'll be back." When he'd gone the stable seemed unnaturally quiet, and Blossom laid her head down with a sigh. Kitty rustled across towards her, crouched where Jack had been, and put out one very shy, tentative hand. The mare rolled her great eyes so the whites showed, then closed them in resignation as Kitty stroked her mane.

"I don't think you need to worry," she said. "I'm pretty sure Jack knows what he's doing; he seems to know a lot about horses." There was an awkward pause, which she filled in by patting the side of Blossom's head. She wished she knew how you were supposed to talk to animals. Baby talk didn't seem right for Blossom – she was such a formidable creature, infinitely more experienced than Kitty. She was a lot more familiar with Jack, too; it was stupid to have told her he knew about horses. If anyone was aware of that, it was Blossom. How much of what you said were animals supposed to understand, anyway?

"I'll tell you one thing," she went on, her voice sounding too loud, "he'd be a lot less worried if it was me lying there and you were the one doing the head-patting." She was just summoning the courage to say something complimentary about the foal when Jack returned with a pile of equipment and set her to stitching four sacks together with fine cord.

"What are you going to do?" she asked, as he hooked a pulley-wheel to a ring in the ceiling.

"I'm pulling her up. It's that big push she can't manage. If I do it for her and she feels the ground under her feet she might take a turn for the better."

"Why can't she just lie there till she feels stronger?" Blossom definitely looked as if that was what she'd prefer to do.

"Because she'll get water on the lung if she stays down too long." Jack looked critically at Kitty's sewing. "It don't have to be that fancy," he said.

"I want to do a good job," she answered stiffly. "There's no point in being slapdash."

"Funny little hands you've got," he said, catching hold of one. "Why don't you paint your nails? I like scarlet ones, they're sexy."

Kitty pulled her hand away, annoyed by his cockiness. "You'd be lucky to get me as I am."

"I would and all," he said quietly, his voice no longer teasing, and began threading a rope through one of the pockets she'd made. She bent her head and sewed faster, confused by his abrupt change of mood. He was such an odd mixture of arrogance and sweetness.

When the sling was ready they had to roll Blossom to one side, push it under her, and roll her back. On the second roll there was a sharp crack, and Kitty felt a tickle run up the inside of her leg; her tight jeans had finally given up. She didn't care; she'd been getting increasingly annoyed by the way they restricted her movements. She'd get some loose ones instead, more suitable for rolling carthorses around in. Blossom, lethargic and floppy, submitted to being pushed with an air of weary sadness.

"Have you called the vet?" Kitty asked suddenly.

"I just rang him. He'll come when he can; he said to try her with a jab of the old man's antibiotic and keep her warm." Jack's skill as a doctor impressed her: his actions were swift and economical, and Blossom didn't notice the dab of surgical spirit on her neck, the slap which followed it, or the hard jab of the needle.

"Have you done that before?"

"Are you having me on?" Jack capped the syringe and tucked it back in his pocket. "I'd given half-a-dozen jabs before I was ten. You can't run a farm without a needle. It'd be a graveyard else, wouldn't it? At least the old man's pig house would be. You can't help feeling sorry for the plonkers that have to eat his pork."

Kitty held the sling steady while Jack fed its central rope through the pulley-wheel. "Pug swears the best way to get a horse to his feet is to pee in his ear, but I don't think Blossom's in the mood for that. I'll pull her up slow instead." He tightened the rope and pulled, so the veins stood out on his temples and his joints crackled. Blossom rose perhaps half an inch. Jack tied the rope up to the manger and rested, breathing deeply. Kitty noticed that the sock on his hand had a fresh bloodstain coming through.

"You'll hurt yourself. It's too hard for you," she pleaded. "Why don't I ask your dad to help?"

Jack slipped the rope free again and pulled, resting occasionally to catch his breath. "He wouldn't be any use. He'd just stand there and tell me I was doing it all wrong. How when he were a lad they did this and did that. No thanks. I don't want to have to hear that cack now. I just want to get on."

Kitty couldn't bear to watch. She stared down at the floor, but hearing it all was just as bad: the scrape of Blossom's hooves on the floor, Jack's laboured breathing and the creak of the pulley. She went and stood beside Jack, holding the rope and pulling when he did, although she doubted she was much use. She felt ashamed of how weak and unfit she was. When the rope went taut she'd pull as hard as she possibly could, so the world narrowed to a blurred red circle and all she was aware of was the rope burning her hands and sweat running into her eyes, but it didn't seem to make much difference to the speed with which Blossom jerked upwards. She came limply, with a squeak of the pulley, looking like a string puppet without its animator, her giant hooves dangling.

Jack stopped to rearrange Blossom more comfortably in the sling, giving her mane a soothing caress. Kitty was glad of the break; he didn't rest long enough between each pull for her liking. He ripped off his shirt with one swift movement and wiped his face with it. The muscles on his arms stood out in bunches; she'd never before seen anyone close to who looked like that, and always thought the idea of super-fitness a little grotesque and ridiculous. It looked all right on Jack, though. His skin was creamily thick, and folded a little round his neck when he hunched his shoulders, like the coat of a wild cat.

She'd stopped even trying to pull by the time he decided the sling was high enough. She faced the stable wall, her hands on its cool bricks, taking deep, rasping breaths.

"That's the best I can do," he said, his voice hoarse. "I might as well have saved me strength; it hasn't worked." Now Blossom was almost completely upright it was obvious how little spirit she had left: her eyes were shut, her lips brushed the ground, and her legs were folded back at the first joint. Jack set each foot squarely on the floor, and raised her head, but she wouldn't open her eyes. "Cruel, that's what I am," he murmured, and very carefully lowered her back to the floor. Kitty slid to the ground and watched while he fluffed straw up behind Blossom's head and covered her body with the sling. Then he sat beside the mare, took her great head in his lap, and stroked her mane and ears, pulling them through his fingers, his eyes vague. His skin looked dark next to the white mane; Kitty saw the mare's eyes open a crack, and a line of eye gleam. She'd never noticed before that Blossom had a moustache, a stiff, bristly one, parted neatly into two halves; it seemed irreverent to be aware of it now. She hesitated before she spoke, thinking Jack might not be in the mood to talk, but then she remembered from the cart ride that when he didn't feel like conversation he simply refused to make it, so she ventured the question:

"What are you going to do, I mean with your life?"

"Stay here," he answered sleepily.

"Why don't you get a job? You don't like working with your dad, do you?"

"Who'd have me?" Jack's voice sounded amused. "I ain't got any CSEs and you need them for anything, even cleaning up pig shit."

"You could go to night school and get some."

"Oh yes. I can see meself doing that. Fit in well with all this, wouldn't it? No, I'll stick it out here. It's the only way I can keep the horses, and they're all I care about. I'll put up with the old man. He's not too bad, I can handle him." She heard him patting Blossom. "What about you?" he asked. "I dare say you'll be moving on soon."

Kitty began trying to explain her situation. The stable seemed wrapped in a blanket, she could hear no sounds from outside, and beyond their faint cone of light, falling only on the last two stalls, it was sootily dark. It was like those evenings she used to spend lying on her bed, talking to schoolfriends on the telephone; she wasn't afraid to be honest. The trouble was, she seemed to be talking about somebody completely different from her, whose behaviour was ridiculously childish and self-pitying. And she ran into odd areas of difficulty when she began to discuss Lance. For a start, she was sick of his name, and disliked even saying it, it sounded so namby-pamby; she wished he'd had a rugged, masculine name, like Armstrong or Butch, then she was sure she would have found it easier to explain to Jack how fatally attractive she'd found him. It seemed impossible to give a convincing reason why she'd ever had anything to do with him at all. Jack tried to help her by prompting.

"Handsome, was he?"

"No – not *really*. Interesting; a clever face."

"Clever," Jack said, as if that was explanation enough. There was a pause, while she framed a reply about everyone having different abilities of equal worth. She felt it was vital to avoid being patronising.

"He sounds a right plonker to me," Jack said unexpectedly, as she was opening her mouth to begin.

It seemed to round off the story of her emotional blunder with awesome accuracy.

"You see," she said, "when you're involved with an older man, and he tells you something, about, well, how you ought to behave in bed, or just generally in a relationship, it's like holy writ, it goes straight into your brain and you don't think of questioning it. At least I didn't."

Jack said nothing, and since she wanted to prolong the conversation and keep him company until the vet came she began talking about her hopes for the future. "I don't really know what I'm going to do," she said. "When I try doing things I like for money they get spoiled. I really loved cooking before I started in catering. Everyone used to tell me what talent I had. But

148

now it's all mixed up with using disgusting ingredients and trying to please silly people like Mayonne Ridley.

"You know, when I was a child I used to spend my whole time reading fairy stories. I liked them so much because you could tell what was going to happen right from the beginning, and I've always hated suspense. Also, I loved the way simple virtues like obedience and hard work were always rewarded. You don't have to be clever or sophisticated to end up with what you want if you're a heroine in a fairy story; you only have to be persistent.

"But there was one story that really upset me. I kept trying to think up better endings for it, rewrite it in my mind. It was the one about Rumpelstiltskin. Do you know it?" She looked across at Jack. His eyes were wide open, she saw them glitter, but he wasn't looking at her, he was gazing at the opposite wall.

Kitty carried on, but she couldn't stop her voice sounding artificial, as if she was talking to herself. "It's a story about a peasant's daughter who gets a reputation for being able to spin straw into gold. She can't really, but the king doesn't know that. He likes gold, so he imprisons her in a dungeon full of straw and tells her if she doesn't transform it she'll be killed. She's quite desperate, and then this horrible-looking little dwarf appears and offers to do the job for her in exchange for her bracelet. Anyway, the story goes on for some time, as fairy tales do, the dwarf arriving every night to turn the straw into gold; and the stakes keep getting higher. By the end the king is offering the girl marriage if she spins the straw, and the dwarf wants her first-born child as a reward. She ends up with everything she wants – married to the king and with a baby – trying to get out of her promise to the dwarf. There's a long section where he very decently agrees to release her if she discovers what his name is, and she manages it, and he has a fit of rage and dies.

149

"It's a peculiar story, isn't it? So unfair to the dwarf. I didn't understand it for a long time; I avoided reading it because I found it so distressing. The dwarf may have looked horrible, but that was no excuse for treating him badly, and he was much kinder than the king. But once I realised the story was about talent it all fell into place. I've never heard a better description of talent than 'turning straw into gold', have you? That's what it is: taking basic materials, available to everyone, and turning them into something precious and unique. The dwarf stands for that invisible extra person who seems to help you achieve the almost impossible. You know, you often don't feel it's you that's done it, that it's come from somewhere else. And it's completely right that the peasant girl should end up betraying the dwarf when she becomes successful – because that's what seems to happen to everyone who ever makes it in life. That's why I don't really care if I don't make anything of myself."

She felt tears in her eyes when she'd finished. She sat silently against the wall, and Jack turned to her and said:

"You're right about it being apart from you. I feel that. When I got me first match plough I couldn't set it up proper, and none of the old horsemen I asked'd show me how. It wasn't in their interest to, was it? It's real hard, setting a plough, and I was working mine with Blossom and a horse I'd borrowed off Eli, buggering about trying to get it to come right, when I felt like there was a hand helping me. I'd change the coulter and not know why I'd done it, but the furrow'd cut cleaner."

"What's it like, working with Blossom?"

Jack clasped the long white head more tightly and leaned forward. "There's nothing to match it," he said. "She guesses what I'm going to do before I think it meself. I don't have to use reins with her, she does it all with the voice. And it hasn't been easy for her, getting like that. See, other animals is only doing what comes natural when they works for you. Sheepdogs, they've an instinct to round creatures up before you start to train them, and horses race each other for a pastime, so it's no hardship to them to run the Grand National. But a heavy horse never does anything like carrying shafts or pulling carts in nature. That couldn't be farther from what they feel easy with. You're asking them to do hard, unnatural work, just to please you. And a good horse'll go down on her knees and burst her heart before she gives up." He looked down at Blossom. "I'll never find her equal," he whispered. "Where's that pissing veterinary to?"

"Do you want me to go and ring him again?"

"If you like."

When she got back Jack was sitting in the same position and the foal had crept in beside him and gone to sleep.

"He'll be here in half an hour," Kitty said excitedly. "He was just waiting for the snow ploughs to get through. He said if you're worried to give her another injection." There was no response, so she added, "I told him we were keeping her warm and he said he was sure she'd get better. They often have an adverse reaction after a difficult foaling; well, you said the same, didn't you?"

Jack looked up at last. "I can do without him now," he said quietly. "She's up and died on me, hasn't she?"

"But she can't have! You got all the afterbirth out and she was getting better! Besides, I liked her, I don't want her to be gone."

Jack gazed steadily at her, his eyes dry, and she knew he only wanted her to leave him alone.

12

The vet arrived at mid-morning. Kitty had been sniffing into a paper hanky since first light, and the three men were sitting stolidly round the kitchen table, mugs of tea cooling before them. Jack acted as if the rest of the world had become muffled and distant and it was only by concentrating extra hard that he could make sense of it at all. If either of the other two spoke he'd watch them carefully, eyes wide and intent, his gaze lingering long after they'd finished, and his own voice sounded rusty from disuse. When the news of Blossom's death was broken to Pug his head had rocked back on his short, crinkly neck, and he'd sucked in his lips with a sound like a sneeze in reverse. The general consensus was that it was a bad business. No one actually voiced the opinion that the vet was at fault, but you could see it hovering almost palpably above their heads.

"Could have been a twisted gut. I've known that happen before now," Pug was conceding generously, putting the case for the defence, as the car drew up. A willowy individual climbed out, wearing a pair of long green waders. He was exactly the type of person Kitty's parents would have asked to a dinner party: he had the right blend of kindly intelligence and marginal physical decrepitude. While obviously not much over thirty, he had pronounced baldness, a pot belly the size of a bowler hat straining against the zipper of his puffa jacket, and skin which was pink round the edges with anxiety. He'd glanced up at the window, caught Kitty's eye, and smiled, and she couldn't help smiling back; he had a likeable face.

All four men walked up to the stable with the mock-reluctant haste, the air of "let's get this over fast; I'm a busy man" that punters assume as they approach a Soho striptease parlour, but when they came back again half an hour later they looked like pall-bearers at a funeral and the vet wasn't swinging his bag any more. It was obvious that he'd been proved at fault and the autopsy had revealed a piece of septic afterbirth.

"You'll have a drink," Roger told the vet severely when he'd finished washing his hands at the sink. The man quivered and sat down, sipping reluctantly at a tumblerful of the Cyprus sherry that shared a greasy pigeonhole in the dining room sideboard with two bottles of HP sauce. Kitty felt sorry for him, until he began speaking. He had a pleasant educated voice, and she winced when she heard it. Did she really talk like that? Jack had said she did, so she must. The vet sounded as if he was talking through a narrow cardboard tube, and he scarcely opened his lips at all, only occasionally dropping the lower one to reveal bottom teeth crushed up and fighting for space. He spoke soothingly of the problems of making a diagnosis at long range, and of getting anywhere fast in a blizzard. There was an air of unimpeachable fairness about his words, and Kitty couldn't see why Jack didn't spring up and throttle him. Instead he stared into his face with painful intensity, and the two older men made sympathetic noises like "Oh yes?" and "That'd be right, then."

When the vet had climbed into his car and driven away, Kitty said passionately, to no one in particular, "You shouldn't have let him get away with that! It was his fault Blossom died, wasn't it? You should take him to court and get him to pay damages." Pug winced and Jack looked away, and it was Roger who answered her.

"No, that's never right. Best leave it be. Only ones to get fat out of court cases is lawyers; besides, where there's live stock, there's dead stock, you've to expect a bit of misfortune."

"But he'll do it again to someone else."

"That he won't. We caught him on the hop at that there autopsy, caught him good and proper. It wouldn't surprise me if he was to leave the county altogether. That sort always run at the first sniff of trouble."

"Stallion got his own back." Pug said suddenly. "While we was off up to the stable with the veterinary I saw he come round by the gate. Had a weird set to his head, he did, like he knew there was trouble, and he trotted up to that there fancy car and bit off the wing mirror. Spat it out after, I saw it on the ground as we was coming back."

She didn't hear any more because a migraine crept up on her and absorbed all her attention. It was the first she'd had since arriving at Balls Farm, and it began, as they all did, with transparent fingers waving at the periphery of her vision. A fellow student had told her that frustration and swallowed rage gave you migraines, and this one certainly bore out the theory. When the fingers became rippling zigzags in front of her eyes, so that it was like looking through a shallow stream, she crept upstairs and hid in her bed; if she could only get to sleep it might all finish before the headache began. She didn't have any of her medicines with her, but they were all useless anyway. They just tasted of cheap, stale chocolate and accelerated the feeling of nausea.

It proved quite impossible to get to sleep: vehicles kept driving into the yard and reversing with difficulty, getting their wheels stuck in the snow. There'd be formless shouts of encouragement, then, that vibrated against her brain like a dentist's drill, and she'd be unable to resist the temptation of looking out through the curtains to see what was happening. Once it was a stoutish woman in jodhpurs bouncing down from a horse-box and helping Jack push Blossom's skittering, nervous foal into the back. Another time she'd seen an open flat-bed lorry slalom through waves of brown slush with a white body dripping blood in the back. She'd had to get up then, and run for the bathroom, and by a stroke of extraordinary good fortune Mrs Ridley wasn't occupying it at the time.

Then there was Lancelot. When the lorries had stopped revving back and forth, and the men had dispersed to quieter activities Lancelot took over the key role of tormentor. She first heard his questioning, nattering cry at two o'clock, the time she usually fed him. This cry became stronger and more irritable, until she could hear, with quite supernatural clarity, the scuffling noise he made as he jumped up at the sides of his pen. There was a long silence while she thought about going downstairs, warming a nauseous saucepan of milk, funnelling it into a slimy bottle, and watching it glug down Lancelot's pulsating red throat. She'd just come to the conclusion that it was probably time he was weaned anyway, he was far too stout to need three pints of milk a day, when the baaing began again, far louder than before. In fact it seemed to be right outside her bedroom window. She looked blearily through the glass, but couldn't see anything. (It would have been hard to; her migraine had reached the stage where all she could see was a dense green film, sometimes broken by random bubbles of clarity.) Lancelot's voice was now sharply angry, occasionally muffled, as if by an eiderdown, only to re-emerge with all its former vigour. "Aargh, aargh, aargh," he bawled, and frequently "narg" as the eiderdown descended. Often, too, there'd be a snapping, crackling noise, What *was* he up to? She'd have to get up soon; it must be nearly time to cook the evening meal. The thought sent her racing to the bathroom.

The gaps in the larder were periodically filled by someone with very muddy footprints and odd tastes. A long time ago the swedes, which had shrivelled to the size and texture of shrunken heads, had been replaced by cabbages, a fresh sack every week, brimming with beads of dew and an enthusiasm she couldn't reciprocate. The luncheon meat had been supplanted by a job lot of cans, stamped 'Eat before May 1953' and labelled FISKE BOLLER: NORWEGIAN FISH BALLS. She'd opened one out of curiosity and found strange white globes inside, floating in brine. They were the exact colour and texture of hard-boiled eggs, except of course, that there was no yolk, and they tasted, despite the brine, of absolutely nothing. Although she privately agreed with the purchaser that this was a superb guesthouse food, she hadn't dared serve it to Mayonne. There wasn't a freezer at Balls Farm, it wouldn't have been possible to run one with no electricity at night, so it was a choice, each day, of tinned meat or whatever strange joint had materialised in the fridge. This morning Kitty had found something which described itself, on a thrillingly attractive packet, as 'slices of rare roast beef in a rich gravy' and inside resembled a large colostomy bag, filled with brown matter. It was the thought of snipping this open and squeezing it out on to a plate that made her falter.

She stumbled downstairs and opened the back door. When she squinted and shut one eye she could see Lancelot gobbling at the ivy that covered the front of the house, his fat tail twirling with pleasure. He'd managed to clear a strip of leaves nearly a metre high along the whole of the back wall, so Balls Farm now looked as if it was wearing a green coat that had shrunk in the wash.

"Lancelot!" she shouted, nearly cracking her head open with pain, and he pranced gaily up to her and peed. He always did that when he saw her; she'd thought it ill-mannered at first, until she'd realised it was a sign of affection. She'd miss it now, if he stopped. "You're a very naughty lamb," she whispered, and tottered back into the house to get his milk. The powdered kind had run out days ago; now she gave him fresh milk from the larder. He didn't wait politely outside, as she'd hoped, he did a brief Fred-Astaire-type dance routine over the front step, skipping with his legs held stiff, sprang at the dog, and leapt back in exaggerated horror when it lifted its head. The dog's horror was real. He gave a howl and scrabbled for the safety of the kitchen.

When Kitty had fed Lancelot and imprisoned him back in the sheep shed she sat for some time with her head in her hands, groaning to herself, and wondering how she'd find the courage to cook dinner. The dog kept her company, sniffling under the table, and they both moved guiltily to the stove when the three men returned. Kitty tried to decide what to serve with the beef. She had to avoid anything that made her feel queasy or required a sharp movement, particularly of the head. If she kept it very still and swivelled it slowly, the headache was bearable and the nausea remained well below danger level, like a diesel-tainted sea slopping against the piles of a rotting pier. She decided to start with grapefruits, cut them with no particular difficulty, and placed them on the dining-room table. It wasn't going to be too pleasant opening tins, but at least that way she wouldn't have to peel anything. She thought of asking Jack for help, but he was sitting sadly beside Pug, and she couldn't catch his eye.

"Did I ever tell you about the time Norman went wood-cutting?" Pug asked, rousing himself from torpor. "There were an old oak what the council wanted to be rid of, down by the river, and Norman put in a tender for it and got the job. He took little Ike along to help with the work; you know Ike, soft in the head, but a good hard worker. Only man I know who can bite an apple in two with his gums." Pug warmed to his story now, oblivious of the fact that each member of his audience was wrapped in a private woe. Kitty was finding the dog's position in front of the stove a little inconvenient. She couldn't set any plates to warm in the lower oven because his bottom was in the way. "It were a misty day, and Ike, he were acting cracked, capering and singing scraps of old songs, supped too much cider the night before, I reckon. Thirsty, too, he were, kept stopping to drink water from his cap. He goes round the other side of the tree, to hold the saw steady . . . "

Kitty heard the guests sit down in the dining room, and she pulled the bag of beef out of its saucepan.

" . . . When all of a sudden Norman sees blood dribbling from the teeth of the saw. Well, straight away he thinks it's Ike, see, messing about and got caught, but

then he hears a shout behind him and sees Ike, fit as a flea, drinking river water. So he thinks to his self, 'Where's this blood to?' Gravy oozed between the blades of Kitty's scissors. Despite the nausea-potential of Pug's story, she was grateful for it; it had certainly taken her mind off the beef. "So he pulls his self up into the tree and looks down, and what does he see?" Pug paused dramatically before shouting "Bats! Hibernating bats! Millions upon millions of them, big black bastards, jammed in there so tight they couldn't fly out again. And they was all squishy with their own blood . . . "

The bag of meat jerked in Kitty's hands and the slices shot out in a thick wedge and landed neatly on the dog's head. He didn't appear to notice; it was the gravy that woke him up.

"Look what I've done!" Kitty wailed, as the dog sprang to his feet, the meat hanging off one ear like a beret.

"Keep your hair on," Roger said soothingly, picking

the meat off with his fingers. He handed it back to her. "Pop a dash of gravy on top and no one'll be the wiser."

"I can't do that!"

"Of course you can. I'm not having you throw out good meat in my house. Besides, a bit of dog hair never did anyone any harm. We all got to eat a peck of dirt before we dies."

Kitty obeyed him, clapped a hand over her mouth, and fled upstairs. Hours later, when the headache was only an irritation, she went downstairs to cope with the washing-up. It had already been done, and a note in Mr Jiggins's handwriting was pinned to the dishcloth. "Thank you for a delicious dinner. Loved the beef!!!" From which she inferred, quite rightly, that Mayonne had made a fuss.

13

"I'll talk to the maid," Roger muttered uncomfortably. Kitty could hear Mrs Ridley's harsh voice echoing off the walls of the milking parlour.

"I've tried telling her before, when there were animal hairs in the butter, but she did not take a blind bit of notice. Obviously she just has not got the same standards as the rest of us. Thinks incompetence is amusing. You'll find this hard to believe, Mr Snell, but when I've tried to set her straight, gone to the trouble of explaining to her in some detail what it is that she's done wrong, thinking it was simply a matter of ignorance, or defective upbringing, I've actually seen a smile on her face. I ask you, what is one to do with a person like that?"

"I'll give her a good talking-to, never you mind." Roger's quiet, comforting replies only goaded Mayonne to further outbursts of irritation. Kitty was listening from the sheep shed, where she was feeding Lancelot his morning bottle. She'd seen Mayonne swing briskly across the yard, wearing a lavender tweed ensemble, and suspecting she was about to complain about the roast beef, moved closer to the open door to listen. Lancelot finished his bottle with a sound like water draining out of a bath, and butted at her knees for more. When she didn't respond he frisked out across the yard and resumed eating the ivy. Only this time, because he'd eaten everything up to nose-level, he had to stand on his hind legs.

"I'm afraid a talking-to isn't enough, Mr Snell. The fact is, your establishment is very far from what I'm accustomed to. The general standard of hygiene is offensive, and the cooking is worse. I have to tell you I'm seriously considering making other arrangements for myself and Miss Biffen. Yours isn't the only guesthouse in the village, you know."

She tapped back to the farmhouse, tossing her stiff hair, carefully combed for the occasion, and Kitty leaned against the shed door and watched her disappear. She felt pleasantly sluttish in her yellow jumper with the gravy stain down the front, the dirty feeding-bottle in her hand.

Roger came to the door of the milking parlour, frowning and pushing his lips in and out, and Kitty waited, smiling slightly, for him to mention the beef, but he didn't. He considered the freshly washed concrete, and would no doubt have gone back inside the parlour without saying anything at all, if Lancelot hadn't snapped off a branch of ivy.

"It's high time that there lamb were weaned," he shouted. "I'm not having him puffing his self out on my good milk. He's a fat nuisance and it wouldn't grieve me to see the back of him. I'm sick of the sound of his voice: moan moan moan. He can stay out in the field with the others." He grabbed Lancelot round the middle, carried him over to the fence, and dropped him into the meadow beyond. "There," Roger said, dusting off his hands. "Proper job. And it's time you got on with the breakfasts, young lady, I've been hearing complaints about you."

Obviously this outburst wasn't sufficient to tap the reserves of irritation left by Mayonne Ridley. Kitty could hear Roger complaining to himself out in the yard, making a low humming sound, and he was so ill-humoured when he came through the back door that he even forgot to congratulate the dog on his goodness and intelligence. He was like an angry wasp looking for someone to sting, and inevitably his eye lit on Jack.

"It might turn out for the best after all," he said, "this business with Blossom. What you wants to do, my lad, is sell that there useless stallion, pay the maid back what you owes her, and put the balance to a half-dozen decent calves. We've the housing for them out back, and they'd give you a good start in farming, teach you the whys and wherefores. It's time you give up all this nonsense about horses and put your back into some solid hard work for a change."

Jack was eating, chewing each mouthful with care, and he put down his knife and fork and pushed the plate away. "He's not your stallion," he replied. "So why don't you shut your face?"

"He's not yours either, is he? Half of him's the maid's. And it's not your hay and your grass that he's eating, neither. What have you to say to that, eh?" Roger was leaning forward, his face flushed with excitement, and when Jack didn't immediately reply he said "eh?" again, the word jabbing into the silence.

"Why don't you come right out with it and say why you don't like the horses?" Jack spat back. "Never had any time for Blossom neither, did you? Tried to stop her being given me in the first place. Why was that, then? Didn't you want me to have a good time? Was that it? Didn't you like another man giving me what I wanted? Or was it the old lady's nose you was trying to get up? Come on then, you might as well come out with it. I'm waiting."

The two men stared at each other across the table.

"I don't have to explain meself to you," Roger said, pulling back his chair and getting up. "Not in me own house and on me own farm. It's you that should be standing there telling me," he banged his fat fist on the

162

table, "what it is you're going to do about this stallion. Stallions without mares," he said, stamping out to the dog's room. "Plain stupid, that is."

Jack watched him go, his fingers curled. "I can't eat any more," he said, not looking at Kitty. "It'd stick in my throat."

"Jack . . . " she began, but he brushed past. She saw him pulling up his coat collar in the yard, and as he climbed into the tractor he had the air of a sheriff in a spaghetti Western readying himself to duff up a posse of bandits.

Kitty began to tidy up. After a migraine all her senses were almost unbearably sharp; it was like looking at the world through a too-strong pair of spectacles and strapping amplifiers to your nose and ears, and the dining room was the wrong place to be. Watery sunshine was trickling through the smeared window-panes, highlighting the pools of fat on the breakfast dishes, and a shaft slid under the sideboard and illuminated what looked like a tiny island, floating on a sea of dust. It reminded Kitty of a watercolour her father had once painted of the Isle of Wight: a low, bumpy coastline rich with purples and greens and the occasional blob of burnt sienna. She knew exactly what it was without looking closer: the dog had been sick.

She'd finally had enough of being a bad housekeeper. She was tired of Mrs Ridley's disapproval, tired of the way life went on getting steadily worse all the time, and this house grimier and grimier. It all seemed linked, a compound mass of failure, stemming from her inability to deal with the central issues of any problem. Well, this was one situation she could change. If she was clever enough to be accepted by one of the top English departments in the country, she was surely capable of spring-cleaning Balls Farm. She forced the front door open with punches and kicks and carried all the carpets and furniture out onto the frozen lawn. Lancelot surveyed the operation with interest from his field, and baaed with approval whenever she appeared on the doorstep. She began by cleaning the floors according to the standard Army camp method: you sloshed boiling water and soda across, put on a stout pair of Wellingtons, and scootered enthusiastically about on the back of a brush. When she'd finished the house looked as if it had been hit by a flash flood; it was time for the fine-detail work. She wiped all the paintwork down with soap and disinfectant, relaid the carpets, and scrubbed them. To her surprise housework wasn't a disagreeable or even a dull job when you did it this way. Each time she flung another bucket of filthy water down the drain she felt she was emptying secret pockets of bitterness deep inside herself and letting in sunshine and sweet air.

Why hadn't anyone ever told her how fulfilling cleaning could be? It was the only way you could be sure of altering your surroundings for the better. There was no agonising about whether you were talented, or other people liked you: either you scrubbed hard enough or you didn't, it was as simple as that. The dining-room wallpaper was actually quite a pleasant pale pink colour, when you scoured all the red fuzz off; which was lucky, because the curtains were pink too when they came out of the tumbledrier. They no longer dragged irritatingly on the floor, either, they were a fashionable three-quarter length, and let in much more light.

After lunch, which neither of the men came in for, Kitty set heaters all over the house to dry it and started polishing the furniture. She was glad she had all those table-legs to do, because it kept her below the level of the windows; Lancelot was feeling hungry now, and whenever he caught a glimpse of her he'd stop grazing with the other sheep and express himself forcefully on the evils of early weaning. Cleaning was really a whole philosophy in itself, Kitty thought, spraying liquid wax over the bottom of the grate and rubbing it to a shine: a matter of making the best of whatever lean resources were to hand, and learning to value even the most ugly, useless items. There was an agreeable spice of martyrdom to it too. She couldn't think why the cult had died out and people were so reluctant to do cleaning nowadays. The answer came to her as she braved Lancelot's displeasure to stretch a crisp, new cloth across the dining-room table. Of course, it was the thought of having it all spoiled immediately you'd finished. She knew that wasn't going to happen here, but it was different in the average home, where spring-cleaning was as rewarding as painting a masterpiece and letting a pack of baboons jump on it afterwards. Paying guests weren't like ordinary people, at least hers weren't. They couldn't make normal dirt. They left mysterious stains on linen, but otherwise made rooms cleaner by passing through them. Why, she had often remarked how brightly the bath shone, with no trace of brown ring, after Mayonne had been standing quietly beside it for a couple of hours.

Years ago, when householders used to scrub the stretch of pavement outside their front doors, they'd built a sense of achievement into housework by leaving one room untouched and perfect, even in a tiny, over-crowded house: the front parlour. If the world would only take up front-parlourism again and return to being house-proud what benefits would accrue! Depression and boredom would be eliminated at a stroke. The beauty of it was that this time round men could share in the psychological benefits too. She had only the haziest idea of social history and couldn't recall reading anywhere that women had actually been happier when they'd done more housework. Perhaps there was a flaw in her reasoning. It was sad, but there usually was, whenever she thought of a really convincing theory.

It was just after five now, and she ought to start the dinner. For the first time her enthusiasm faltered. Her arms were swollen and streaked with dirt, and even after she'd poured all her energy into it, Balls Farm still looked dingy and mean. At least she'd managed to dislodge the doggy smell, replacing it with a toxic smog of furniture polish and ammonia.

When she went into the larder she found six pigeons twirling from a string nailed to the window. She didn't realise what they were at first, because someone had plucked the feathers off, and the soft, bag-like bodies looked strange coupled up to vicious little beaks and toes. They were still warm. Each bird had been shot once through the heart, so it seemed unlikely that Roger was responsible: after reading Deborah May's letters Kitty had the impression he was rather a bungler. Perhaps Jack had killed them. Hadn't she complained to him in the stable about the terrible ingredients she had to work with? If it was him, then the ruthlessness of his aim was a grim indication of his state of mind.

Whoever had provided them, she was grateful for the chance to cook a good meal. She cleaned them and wrapped them in bacon, and planned the rest of the menu while they sizzled in the oven. She'd still have to use packets and tins, but perhaps she could follow Sherry's advice, and please the guests by overloading their plates with food.

When she took the soup into the dining-room – it was the nicest variety, instant French Onion, if you had a bad head cold you wouldn't be able to tell it from real – Mayonne was raising her thin eyebrows at the room, mentally checking off each detail of its transfiguration. She smiled tightly and turned to Miss Biffen.

"I hope you'll agree, Gilly," she said, "that it was worth making a fuss this morning. There's nothing like a good tongue-lashing to bring a slut to heel."

Kitty leapt back into the kitchen as if she'd been

stung. It crossed her mind to throw the pigeons to the dog and open a tin of corned beef instead, but that would hurt her as much as Mayonne. It meant a lot, this one chance to prove herself a decent cook.

She opened the oven and took the birds out. They looked perfect, plump and brown, and using some oval plates she'd found in the back of the cleaning cupboard she laid out the meal as if she was painting a picture. A golden mass of stodge – chips, roast potatoes and batter puddings – enlivened with violent splashes of cranberry sauce and peas, and in the foreground, a triumphant pigeon.

When she set the dishes on the table she glanced round at the guests. It was no exaggeration to say they were stunned. Kitty waited for a word of congratulation but they seemed too awed for speech. Only Mayonne said "Well . . . !" as she left the room.

In the kitchen Roger crackled at his bones, reminding Kitty of a fairy-tale illustration she'd pored over as a child: "the ogre at his dinner". He worked his way through both his portion and Jack's, and Kitty couldn't help feeling sad that Jack wasn't there to benefit from her success. She could hardly swallow her food, she was so excited. After waiting a decent interval, the guests always took far longer than she and Roger did, she opened the dining-room door.

Mr Jiggins had tackled his pigeon with tomato ketchup, nibbling at one end and leaving a pool of clotted sauce round the wound. He was dabbing at his lips now, and taking little sips of water, rinsing away the horrid taste of unprocessed meat. The ladies had made no attempt to eat theirs: Miss Biffen had at least cleared the rest of her plate, but Mayonne had approached the meal as if she was judging it for a competition: the bacon had been unrolled from the bird to check it wasn't concealing any flaws, sections had been taken from each roast potato, and even the batter puddings had been probed and found wanting. She had the habit of leaving a reproach on the side of her plate, a scrap that complained "this carrot was underdone" or "there was too much fat on this bacon," but by rejecting her pigeon dinner outright she was making a stronger statement: "Don't even think of trying to please me, because whatever you do will never be good enough." Kitty cast about for a way of getting back at her.

"Excuse me," she smiled, as she picked up Geoff Jiggins's plate. "But would you mind explaining something?"

"Not at all, Kitty, what would you like to know?" He cleaned the gravy off his moustache with his thumb and forefinger, making a wet snicking sound, and Mayonne winced.

"I just wondered what the little watering can in your room was for," Kitty said sweetly, watching her enemy out of the corner of her eye. She hoped it was for an indescribably rude purpose, the mere elliptical mention of which would make Mayonne choke on her butterscotch whip. She was sorry that Geoff Jiggins was going to be embarrassed, but it would be in the cause of justice.

"I don't in the least mind telling you." Geoff leaned forward eagerly. "For some time now I've been fascinated by the link between the body and the mind, particularly where personal hygiene is concerned. That 'watering can' as you call it, is the heart of my system for flushing out the nasal passages and stimulating the brain." The two ladies gave cries of interest and approval, and as Kitty returned to the kitchen she heard Geoff expounding a theory which mixed cleanliness and religion in a sickeningly familiar manner. "No, it's been of extraordinary benefit to me," he was saying, "literally changed my life. I have a spare can in my suitcase if either of you ladies would care to . . . "

Kitty went upstairs and submerged herself in the bath, washing her hair for the first time in over a fortnight – she preferred it dirty, because then it was flatter. As she dried it she wondered what to do with herself. She'd been a good housekeeper and cook today, yet she felt more miserable than ever. What was the point of all that work if it was only to please people she didn't care for? People who were determined not to be pleased however hard she tried. No matter how she struggled, where she ran to, she always found herself in the same situation: being told she fell short of an ideal she could never hope to achieve. She simply wasn't the right kind of person. Her character was wrong. It was as stupid as her hair. She hated her hair, it fuzzed up on top of her head whenever it could, and stuck out like a rude sign. Maybe her character affected people the same way, making them long to swat her into shape.

She thought back over the six weeks she'd spent at Balls Farm, and the one benefit she could find was that she no longer loved Lance. Her feelings for Lancelot the lamb were stronger: an oddly sweet mixture of exasperation and affection. What about Jack? She shrugged. She thought him very attractive, and had tried hard to understand him and get close to him, but since Blossom's death he seemed to have turned against her. Whenever he was annoyed or unhappy he retreated into himself and avoided her, and she was tired of only ever getting so far with a relationship, of struggling at the gates of a fortress that always left her defeated and in tears. In his own way Jack was as unapproachable as Lance.

What did she feel like doing? Sh'd realised today that there was no future for her in housekeeping. What she'd really like to do was go back to university and start again. The more she thought about it the better idea it seemed. She walked backwards and forwards, too excited to keep still. Why shouldn't she go back?

There was no reason not to, now she no longer cared for Lance. She wouldn't be upset if she saw him with other women, and she'd feel no embarrassment at being taught by him. She wouldn't feel anything at all. At last she could be cool and rational, the kind of person he'd always wanted her to be. Her work might even be improved. Best of all, if she went back she could see her mother and father again. Since reading Deborah May's letters she'd felt more and more guilty about the way she'd treated her own mother. Just before Christmas she'd sent her a postcard telling her not to worry, but this now seemed cruelly inadequate. When she got home she was going to fight her way through the knitting-wool and rediscover the vulnerable personality sheltering behind it.

What date was it now? The twenty-first of March. Why, in a month the summer term would begin. She'd only really have missed one term, and she could make up the work if she tried hard enough. All her mistakes could be wiped out, as if they'd never happened.

She rummaged through her belongings for a clean sheet of paper.

"Dear Professor Billow," she began; it was best to keep the words as formal as possible. "You may remember that last term I expressed the wish to resign my place as a student in your department." (She felt hot at the thought of what she'd put in that letter. She remembered weeping as she pushed it into his pigeonhole; it had been ridiculously sentimental.) "I would now like to reconsider my decision . . . "

14

She left the letter on the hall table to catch the next morning's post, filled an illegal bottle of milk for Lancelot, and ran out to the field. She couldn't see her lamb at first; he'd merged in with the rest of the sheep, and it was only when she called his name that he looked up and began blaring with hunger.

They walked together up the side of the valley, Lancelot stopping occasionally to nibble at the grass. The snow had begun melting, although there were still hard banks of it under the hedges and on the roofs of Balls Farm. The buildings looked almost pretty from up here, now snow blurred their ugly shapes and unsuitable colours. Lancelot crackled through a thorn bush and waited patiently to be released; then he fell down a rabbit hole and had to be hauled out by the back legs. She was just thinking about turning back – the light was fading and pigeons were coming in to roost in the trees – when she saw a dark oblong above her, hanging from the lip of the valley, and decided to investigate. She had to approach it circuitously, the land was marshy here: this must be where the spring surfaced, the one supplying Balls Farm with its uniquely disgusting water, sugary and nearly always brown: "Blooming cows have trod on the pipe again," Roger would say, choking on his tea. Lancelot didn't like getting his feet wet, so she cradled him like a child as she jumped the stepping-stones of coarse grass between the water-weed. He enjoyed the ride: when he felt thirsty he could suck passionately at her earlobe.

The dark oblong proved to be a wedge-shaped boulder, easily ten feet high, embedded in the almost vertical edge of the valley, and perched on top, legs dangling, was Jack. She wondered whether to approach him at first. She told herself it was because she felt it was disrespectful to burst in on his melancholy with a rowdy companion like Lancelot, but really she felt a mixture of fear and reluctance. She was scared that Jack would misinterpret and reject her friendly advances, and was shamefully reluctant to share his grief. She hadn't known either him or Blossom long enough to say the right words of consolation; she knew she'd only sound crass if she tried. She looked up at him. He was gazing into the distance, his mouth drawn down at the corners like a clown's, and on impulse she scrambled up the stone and slid beside him. Lancelot made a nittering sound and frisked up behind her, arranging himself comfortably against her back.

You could see the whole valley from here, the lights of Wormington glowing on the horizon and occasionally a pair of red dots flickering through the trees as a car swept up to the pub at the crossroads. Balls Farm itself was only a few squares of yellow at the bottom of a deep black cup made by the fields, but even so she could hear its generator rattle and fainter yet, the musical babble of the television.

"You can hear it all from here," Jack said suddenly. "Sound bounces straight up the valley, as clear as if you was standing in the yard. You can't hear words, just like the tone of what people are saying." Kitty watched him covertly, uncertain how to reply, and after a while he continued, his voice dreamy: "When I was small I liked to pretend this was a magic stone, and would give

172

me anything I wanted. I'd only have to sit here and wish and it'd all come true."

"Did you ever make a wish?"

"I put it off and put it off. I half believed it all and didn't want to prove meself wrong. But I did ask it the one time, and my wish did come true."

"What happened?"

It was autumn, and he was ten years old, running through the shoulder-high bracken, brambles ripping at his bare legs, his throat so raw it burned each time he drew breath. He could hear muffled shouts behind him, and he struggled up the stone and looked down. Far below, like toys on the floor of his bedroom, he could see the tractor slewed across the drive, and a tiny grey head poking out over the slats in the back of the trailer. The light was on in the kitchen, and angry shadows flickered across the glass. He drew up his knees and bit his knuckle. "Let me keep her! Let me keep her!" He thought the words so loud he felt they'd been shouted, and echoed round the valley. The stone trembled beneath him, and he opened his eyes and saw the kitchen window shatter. Then he heard his mother's thin wail, and he wasn't in a magic world any more but back in the nightmare of his dark bedroom, trying not to listen to the shouts from downstairs. He did now what he did then: tried to be like the three china monkeys on his mantelpiece – see no evil, hear no evil and speak no evil – and wrapped his arms round his face, jamming his fingers in his ears so his forearms blocked off his eyes and mouth. So he didn't hear the whoomph! as the stove exploded, or see the flash illuminate the yard, and it was seemingly hours before he dropped his hands and saw the ambulance bounce up the drive, red tail-lights glowing. When he'd crept into the house, sobbing with fear for his mother, she'd seized him in the blackness of the passage and whispered to him that Blossom was his to keep for ever.

173

"Why do you think your dad didn't want you to have Blossom?" Kitty asked. She was careful not to smile. It was odd knowing more of the story than Jack did.

"I don't know. I've had the thought of that evening on my mind the last couple of days, that's why I said what I did at breakfast, but I didn't know he'd take it so hard. Could be he feels it were his fault Pug got hurt."

"Pug?"

"Yes, Pug. He fell against the old stove we had then, and it set fire to the back of his head. That's why he looks so weird. Vain old bugger wears a wig; hair never grew back, see. He and the old man grew up together, best friends they are, so alike if you overheard them talking you'd think it was Pug nattering to his self. The old man'd never have the neck to beat Pug up. Or anyone, come to that; at least not if they was bigger than him."

"So Pug gave you Blossom?"

"Course he did. Haven't you been listening? When I was a kid he was always good to me, kinder than the old man. Far back as I can remember he played with me and give me presents, and when the old lady up and left it's like he took her place, helped me against the old man."

"What did he look like before the accident?"

"I can't remember. They say he was handsome enough. What's it to you?"

Kitty drew back from revealing the truth. She was fond of Roger, and she wanted to believe that his grumpiness concealed some affection for Jack. By telling Jack who his real father was she'd destroy the three-cornered relationship at Balls Farm, and the only person who would benefit was Pug. It was better to leave things the way they were: if Deborah May had wanted Jack told she would have done it herself. "Oh, I don't know," Kitty said. "I was just thinking."

"That's what I was doing before you come up here.

Thinking. I got to wondering if the old man was right or no. I don't seem to have any luck with the horses, and it could be I should sell the stallion and get out of them altogether, like he says."

"Don't you like the stallion any more?" Kitty's tone was fiercer than she'd intended.

"It's not that I don't like him, but all's changed now Blossom's gone. There isn't any point to it any more." He turned to Kitty. "I've to pay you back, for certain."

"I don't want to be repaid. You mustn't sell Truncheon. Promise me you won't. And you mustn't give up either. If you think of Blossom, what Pug suffered to give her to you, and what she and Truncheon went through to learn how to work properly – you can't throw all that away! You know, I think, I'm quite *sure* that there's a reason for everything that happens to us, and maybe you can't see the reason for Blossom dying now but I'm sure you will one day. You've got a talent for working horses, you know you have. You said so to me yourself. If you gave it all up now you'd always regret it." She felt hot tears on her cheeks. "You've got to listen to me," she said, "because when things seem hopeless in your life you can't always see the way out of them yourself. You're the worst person to decide."

Jack touched her cheek. "Why are you crying?" he asked.

"Because I'm stupid," she replied, wiping the tears away quickly with a finger.

"Go on – tell me why."

"I suppose it's just . . . I made the same mistake as you. I got out of something I ought to be doing because of an emotional reason. I should have stopped to think." She swallowed. "I've decided to go back to university and start again."

She climbed off the boulder and began walking downhill.

175

"I thought you didn't think much to the place," Jack replied, draping Lancelot round his neck and following

She sniffed a little. "It wasn't university that was wrong for me, it was that man."

"That's different, is it?"

"What do you mean?"

"He's your teacher, isn't he? Isn't that going to make life a little hard?"

"I'll manage."

"See, I'm different from you," Jack said. "I'd sooner trust the way I feel than the way I think."

"You're quite wrong. That's the way to make terrible mistakes."

"What, and all these thinkers you're so keen on, they don't make mistakes?" She could tell he was smiling.

"Well, of course they do sometimes. Even if you think hard you can't always . . . They don't make such *bad* mistakes, that's the answer."

"I reckon the others have more fun along the way." Jack put Lancelot down and scooped Kitty up in his arms.

"What are you doing?" she squeaked.

"I'm getting you over the sheep netting. We're back at the farm."

Kitty looked round. They were outside Jack's house, and she could hear the ten o'clock news ending. Any minute now Roger'd announce grimly to the assembled guests, "Some of us has to work tomorrow," struggle out of the soft armchair he'd been in all evening, and give the animals a final check. Then without any warning whatever, he'd snap off the generator, leaving the upstairs corridor full of panicky bodies in dressing-gowns. It had occurred to Kitty that that was how ghostly legends got made. Strange, wasn't it, that ghosts were nearly always sighted at the end of dark passageways, clad in flowing robes, and that they vanished when challenged? Maybe there was a simpler explanation than the supernatural: just guests trying to find their way in the dark.

"I have to go now," Kitty said with great dignity, but Jack didn't set her down.

"No you don't," he replied, his voice a little too loud. A sheep coughed disapprovingly nearby, like an old maid in a library. Jack tensed, and Kitty was reminded of the morning she'd watched Truncheon working in the field. He'd frozen like that when he was deciding whether to bolt or not. Kitty knew she had only to say the right words, a little prickly and annoyed, and Jack would release her at once. She didn't want him to, she felt safe in his arms. The delicate line of his jaw was directly in front of her face, and without realising what she was doing she leaned forward and brushed it with her lips. He charged at his chicken house, kicked in the door, and they landed together on the bed with a crash. The two brass ends almost touched above their heads, and there was a prolonged chiming of springs, like the noise a grand piano makes after falling downstairs.

His kiss felt exactly right this time, the only way a kiss should ever be. At first she felt peaceful and contented, lying there so warmly in the dark, then, as the kiss continued, she felt herself beginning to tremble. Jack took his mouth away.

"I hate the dark," he said, and got off the bed. She heard the door shut, and rustling scraping noises as he fiddled with the fire. She closed her eyes. She was surprised he hadn't been swept away by the heat of the moment. Perhaps she ought to reconsider what she was doing, too. She heard the generator grind to a halt, and the shriek of some night bird close to the trees. And another sound, too, a steady chomping, ripping noise. It stopped briefly, and was replaced by a snort, and she realised it was Truncheon, grazing with the sheep. The bed creaked, and Jack began pulling her jersey over her head. He experienced some difficulty; her mother never got sizes right: either her sweaters fitted like a corrugated skin, as this one did, or they drooped to the knee, one arm longer than the other, ideal only for impersonations of Charles Laughton in *The Hunchback of Notre Dame*.

"Don't you want to after all?" Jack asked gently.

She didn't know what she wanted. She was frightened of making love. Wouldn't her life have remained perfect if she'd never gone to bed with Lance? She felt sex was the end of an adventure, that it froze possibilities before they had the chance to develop, and soured her character so she became a tiresome nuisance, endlessly harping on the same unreasonable demands. She opened her eyes to explain all this to Jack, and found the chicken house had turned a rich, golden sepia. An oil-lamp flickered on the television, casting a diffuse browny-yellow fuzz upwards over the gigantic furniture tipping in from the walls, and downwards onto the crumpled white bed where she lay. Jack was beside her, propped on one elbow. He was naked. The light deepened the black of his hair and eyelashes, so that they looked as if they'd been painted on with a fine brush, and made his skin shimmer like bronze. He raised one eyebrow questioningly, his mouth a little sad, and she reached out for him, determined not to disappoint by being prudish or shy.

15

Kitty looked down into the yard. Jack was out there, standing on the cart with Truncheon in the shafts. The stallion looked magnificent now: flesh bulged under his skin and he stood solidly on his massive legs, neck proud and ears pricked, the brilliant sunlight turning his pink plush coat a creamy colour. He was such an odd shape for a horse, so broad and stocky, and his face didn't have the fine boniness of Blossom's: it was just a little like a pig's. But his eyes looked kind and amused, like hers.

He flourished his coarse mane and the harness jingled. Jack glanced over his shoulder at the entrance to the inner yard. "This is the hardest thing for a horse to do," he said. "Backing in shafts. We've been practising round the back, a treat for your last day. Isn't that right, Truncheon?" He was using the horse's name at last, slurring the syllables so that it sounded very like "Trojan".

He clicked his tongue and shook the reins and Truncheon hesitated.

"Back, boy, back," he coaxed, and when that had no result: "Will you do what I say? If I say back I mean back. Don't you show me up now, Truncheon, we're doing this for Kitty. BACK!"

The stallion took a tiny defiant step forward and halted, his oiled hooves glittering. Jack sprang off the cart, came round to Truncheon's head and caught hold of the bridle.

"Don't you start that again!" he said warningly, and pushed at the horse's head.

Kitty rested her elbows on the sill. The window was open and a fresh breeze was blowing in. It was sorely needed. Ever since her spring-cleaning Balls Farm had smelled like an old spongebag, and if you looked carefully you could see white beads of fungus sprinkled across the skirting boards. "He's never going to do it," she called down mockingly. "He's not broken yet."

"He's broke all right," Jack said through gritted teeth. He continued his face-to-face confrontation. All his weight was leaning against the horse now, but Truncheon was too strong to be pushed. He licked Jack on the face.

"Back. Back. Back. Back," Jack said. The stallion raised his head proudly, as if he'd decided the teasing had gone on long enough, and Kitty saw his spine ripple as the centre of gravity shifted. He teetered backwards. "That's the way," Jack said. "That's the way. Keep on back." Truncheon took another step, and another, gradually speeding up until his whole body swayed with the awkward, uncomfortable movement.

The cart rumbled into the inner yard. "Whoa!" Truncheon stopped obediently, and waited, his nostrils flared. "What a good horse! See, it wasn't too bad, was it?" Jack patted his neck and looked up at Kitty. "I told you he'd do it," he said. "They don't take much breaking, these Ardeans horses." He moved his hand along to where the stallion's mane ended, and scratched hard. "You like that, don't you?" he asked teasingly. Truncheon wrinkled his upper lip, nodded his head against his chest, and champed his teeth together in ecstasy.

"Why's he doing that?" Kitty called.

"I've found his tickle-spot. He loves this, can't get enough of it. Horses do it to each other when they're standing in a field: you scratch my back and I'll scratch yours. He's thinking about doing me a good turn, too."

A long patch of shadow fluttered across the concrete and over the cart. Jack smiled up at Kitty. "What are you doing?"

"Packing."

"You got hours yet. Care to come for a ride?"

Kitty looked back at the room. Her suitcase was full and only needed to be squashed shut. On top of the clothes a strip of white paper rustled in the breeze. "With the compliments of Professor L. W. Billow" was printed along the bottom, and across one corner were written the words she knew by heart: "Of course you can come back, Kitty. I never thought you'd stay away." Jack was right: the future wasn't going to be easy.

"Excuse me," asked a diffident voice out in the yard, "but have I come to the right place? This is Balls Farm, isn't it?" A girl stood there, blinking in the sunlight, a rucksack on her back. She was heavier and taller than Kitty, but roughly the same age, with short fair hair blowing across her forehead.

"Can you sort it out, Kitty?" Jack called, uninterested. He began unfastening the chains holding Truncheon to the shafts. "You coming for that ride?"

"I'll be down in a minute."

The girl put out her hand and patted the stallion on the nose. "I love horses," she said. "I used to go riding every Saturday. Would he like a lump of sugar?"

Jack eased the shafts gently to the ground and caught hold of Truncheon's bridle. "I don't give my horses sweets," he growled, "it makes them snappy and spoilt." Kitty smiled a little sadly to herself at the window. It was kind of Jack to put on a grumpy act and save her the pain of feeling jealous on her last day, but she could guess what would happen once she'd gone. Jack clicked his tongue at Truncheon and they clopped off to the stable. The girl watched them go.

"Here," Kitty called, feeling sorry for her. "Do you want to come up? I'll show you round if you like."

"Thanks! How do I get in?"

"Down there where the ivy's shrivelled up. The door in the wall."

"Cheers."

Pug and Roger were sitting in the kitchen, nursing cups of coffee, and the girl had propped her rucksack against the electric stove, and was staring impudently at them. Kitty noticed she had freckles on her nose. Her name was Claire, and she wasn't overly impressed by the house.

"Ooer," she said, when she was shown the dining room, eight places laid at the table.

"There are two families coming in this evening," Kitty said briskly. "I've done the vegetables and made the beds. All you have to do is put the meat in at five. It may look a bit odd, but it'll probably taste okay. By the way, don't use the fish balls unless you're desperate: it's not worth the aggravation." Claire looked at the highly polished sideboard and the starched tablecloths.

"I'll never keep it this clean," she said.

"If you want to know anything, read this little notebook," Kitty continued. "Or you can always ask Mrs Pugh up at the pub. She knows a lot, she's been taking guests for years. And she feels a bit guilty at the moment so she'll do anything she can to help."

"I've never done this before. I don't know how I'm going to manage. Eight people!"

Kitty could hear Pug saying: "Breasts? I love them. You can keep all your thighs and well-turned ankles. It's breasts I like. Big fat breasts." Kitty quickly opened the door to the lounge, and as she ushered Claire through Pug gave one of his barks of laughter. "I wouldn't be surprised if you hadn't found yourself another fancy piece."

"What a disgusting old man," Claire said. "Who's he?"

"Just a friend of the family."

"And what about that boy out there?"

"Mr Snell's his dad."

Claire wrinkled her nose. "They're not much like each other, are they? He's ever so good-looking, isn't he, that boy with the horse?"

"Try and keep it as clean as possible," Kitty said, squishing a button of fungus that was blooming beside the light switch. Claire didn't notice; she was flicking disapprovingly through the naughty calendar.

"They're really sexist, farmers, aren't they?" she said. "What have potato sacks got to do with naked ladies?"

Kitty opened the bathroom door. "The only way to stop guests spending all day in here is not to show them where it is."

Claire dropped the calendar. "Not to show them where it is?"

"Yes. Keep the door shut when they first arrive, and show them the room with the toilet and washbasin, but *don't tell them about the bathroom*. At the end of the first week one of them will probably ask if there happens to be a bath anywhere, and they'll be so grateful when you point it out that they won't dare use it more than once. You'll have the psychological advantage then, you see."

Claire was looking at her as if she was mad. "Why shouldn't they take a bath if they want to?"

"You'll find out." Kitty shut her case and pulled it off the bed. "This is your room, I've got to go now; good luck."

Claire sucked in a breath. "I'm going to need it," she said. "First time away from home!"

Kitty turned on the stair. "Oh – and watch out for Mr Snell. Grab a granny, he would."

As she ran down she thought how much lighter the house seemed without the two ladies in it. They were at

Sherry Pugh's now, and her regime didn't altogether agree with them: they looked fat and pale. Sherry's house rules were certainly inflexible. From eight in the morning until opening time, and from two until four she 'requested politely' that the pub be vacated for cleaning, and Kitty had often seen the ladies in the beer garden, waiting out the hours until they could creep back indoors and squeeze behind another loaded table. It was a minuscule garden, nothing more than two square yards beside the road, its bald turf sprinkled with cigarette stubs and can rings, and the two women would crouch out there on garden chairs, their thick bodies swathed in overcoats and transparent rain hats, chewing indigestion tablets while lorries thundered by in a wash of exhaust. Perhaps they were happy at last, and that was all they'd ever wanted from the country.

Truncheon pulled at the long, lush grass, his halter tied to a fallen tree. The branches above his head sighed like the sea, their leaves luminous and fresh, more lemony than pea green.

"Would your magic stone work for me?" Kitty asked, kissing Jack's warm flesh just below the nipple.

He smiled. "It might. What do you want to ask it?"

"If I can come back."

He shut his eyes. "You don't have to bother. I already done that for you."

"Have you? Have you?" Kitty crouched on top of him, the breeze cold against her naked back, and looked into his face. He wouldn't open his eyes, so she kissed him repeatedly: little tiny kisses all over his nose and cheeks.

"Stop that!" he said, putting his hand up. "It tickles."

"Did you ask it that?"

"I said I did, didn't I? Have I ever lied to you?"

"Yes."

"No I never. When?"

"You said your dad was going to pounce on me."

"He would have and all if I hadn't got there first. We have this arrangement, see, we take it in turns with the housekeepers. He can have little Miss Freckle."

"Really?"

"Really." He pronounced the word with a joke upper-class accent, in imitation of her. "I learned everything I know off a Swedish one what come when I was sixteen. Lovely, she was."

"I didn't mean that; I meant do you really want me to come back?" Kitty regretted the words before she finished saying them. She'd been so proud of herself, this last month, the way she'd kept everything so light and merry. She hadn't made the mistake of telling Jack she loved him. It had been hard; so often it had seemed instinctive to say it; she'd had to bite the words back. But she had been determined to make a success of the few days that remained to her; and now she'd spoilt it all.

"I'm sorry," she said. "I don't want to pester you."

"You're not pestering me." Jack sat up. "I don't mind what you say. There isn't no set of rules."

"Yes there is. There are rules for everything: rules for running guesthouses, and rules for breaking horses. If you make a mistake, you get hurt; that's what the rules are for."

Jack put his arm round her. "When I started breaking Blossom," he said, "I didn't know what the rules were, I made them up as I went along. All I did was follow what I felt was best and try to be as kind as I could along the way. It's up to you to decide what you want. If you had a guesthouse of your own you wouldn't run it like the old man's, and I'm not saying I break horses better than anyone else."

"Human relationships are different," Kitty said. "They're not as simple as ones with animals. You're not being honest if you don't agree. There are things I can't say to you, and probably things you can't say to me."

"Like what? Tell me. Go on, whisper one in my ear. I'll pretend I'm not listening."

Kitty smiled and turned away. "You're silly."

Jack kissed her on the neck, a nibbling, biting kiss, like the ones Lancelot used to give, before he realised she'd definitely stopped feeding him, and wasn't going to change her mind.

"I've got to go," she said, picking up her dress.

"It seems funny to me, you wearing a dress. I've got used to your sweaters. I'll miss them."

"You don't have to. They're staying behind. I've given them all to the dog. He's got a nice soft bed now."

"I'll miss that and all."

"What will you miss?"

"You know what I mean."

"There'll be other housekeepers," she said lightly. "Swedish ones, French ones . . . " She picked up her shoes and ran into the silver-lilac shadow under the trees. "I'll race you back."

Kitty climbed into the market bus with her suitcase, and sat down in the front seat. It was only a single-decker bus, empty except for the driver, who was in his shirtsleeves reading a newspaper. Through the open door she could see Lancelot grazing in the field beside the road. He'd raised his head to watch her as she walked past, but he hadn't run to greet her; he'd stopped doing that long ago.

Kitty had slipped away on her own, leaving Jack unharnessing Truncheon in the stable. Goodbyes were always difficult, and she wasn't sure she could keep this one light enough. It was better just to leave.

The bus driver put down his paper and smiled at her. "Are you fit, then?" he asked, and started the engine.

"Hold on," Jack interrupted, leaning in through the door. "It's not quarter past yet."

Kitty gazed at him. He quite filled the doorway, his curly head touching the ceiling, eddies of musky horse smell swirling around him. He handed her a box with a picture of a sponge-cake on the front; he seemed curiously shy. "I got you a present," he said. "It's not a gold watch, but it's the same colour. It's to make sure you come back; you'll have to, when it gets bigger."

"When what gets bigger?"

"The present." Jack leapt back off the platform, the doors folded shut, and the bus gathered speed down the hill. The box rustled to itself and began piping in a shrill treble. Kitty opened it, fingers trembling. Inside, in a handful of hay, was a scrap of brilliant yellow fluff; it shrank down when it saw Kitty and hissed a challenge through the tiniest orange beak. She laughed, tears in her eyes. "I don't even like geese! And what am I going to do with you at university?" It wasn't until she was on the train, coaxing it to eat a British Rail sandwich, that she noticed the piece of grimy paper it was sitting on. Written across it in spiky handwriting were the words "I love you".

SYLVIA MURPHY

THE LIFE AND TIMES OF BARLY BEACH

Jenny Sharpe takes refuge in unspoilt Barly Beach after the break-up of her ill-judged marriage. After an idyllic summer there with her young son Thomas, she decides to stay and they begin to carve out a place for themselves.

On the whole, life is pleasant and Barly remains a relatively unspoilt backwater until the Black Corporation decides it is time to exploit Barly's potential for redevelopment. But the people who live there aren't prepared to let a bunch of greedy property developers have it all their own way . . .

'Written with subtlety and cunning and every page, sentence and word is completely delightful'

The Daily Telegraph

'Sylvia Murphy's gentle novel provides splendid, unpretentious comedy at the expense of pompous property developers'

The Times

'Ominously entertaining'

The Guardian

A Royal Mail service in association with the Book Marketing Council & The Booksellers Association.

Post-A-Book is a Post Office trademark.

MAVIS CHEEK

PAUSE BETWEEN ACTS

Joan's answer to life-after-divorce is simple: happy seclusion: a citadel of perfect peace and sanity, which takes a little madness to maintain . . .

To stop her parents knowing about the divorce she invents a woman lodger from Nigeria . . .

To keep her ex-husband at bay she invents an affair between herself and the imaginary lodger . . .

Meanwhile she must hold off the dog-like devotion and persistent advances of the young PT teacher from school . . .

Enter, then, the roguishly theatrical Finbar Flynn and despite herself, the walls of her citadel look set to come tumbling down . . .

HODDER AND STOUGHTON PAPERBACKS

FAY WELDON

THE PRESIDENT'S CHILD

Babies have fathers too, and when that father is soon to be President Elect of the U.S., mothers had better beware. When the interests of powerful men conflict with those of intelligent women, who wins?

A stunning parable of our life and times.

'One of the most readable, articulate, and fascinating of contemporary writers'

The Scotsman

HODDER AND STOUGHTON PAPERBACKS

FAY WELDON

LITTLE SISTERS

Elsa's not really very good at typing though she tries. Would she do better as a good-time girl? A weekend in the country with her suave new lover and his millionaire friends proves that life and love are both more magical, and more murderous, than Elsa, or any of us, had ever supposed.

'Delicious, effervescent . . .'

Daily Telegraph

HODDER AND STOUGHTON PAPERBACKS

MORE TITLES FROM
HODDER AND STOUGHTON PAPERBACKS

SYLVIA MURPHY

☐ 49486 7 The Life and Times of Barly Beach £2.50

MAVIS CHEEK

☐ 49747 5 Pause Between Acts £2.99

FAY WELDON

☐ 33965 9 The President's Child £2.50
☐ 23827 5 Little Sisters £2.50